Faith's Destiny 2:

❋

Destiny's Faith

Q Taylor

iUniverse, Inc.
Bloomington

Faith's Destiny 2:
Destiny's Faith

This is a work of fiction. All of the characters, names, incidents, organizations, and dialogue in this novel are either the products of the author's imagination or are used fictitiously.

iUniverse books may be ordered through booksellers or by contacting:

iUniverse
1663 Liberty Drive
Bloomington, IN 47403
www.iuniverse.com
1-800-Authors (1-800-288-4677)

ISBN: 978-1-4759-2867-9 (sc)
ISBN: 978-1-4759-2868-6 (e)
ISBN: 978-1-4759-2869-3 (hc)

Printed in the United States of America

iUniverse rev. date: 05/30/2012

To my father, Big Quen, who taught me patience, coolness, and collectiveness.
He gave me the courage to be different and taught me why it is so important to use our minds, even in our darkest hours.

"You can't be rock star with no guitar."
—Daddy O, a.k.a. O. C. Nixson

Contents

Prelude   xi

Chapter 1:

Faith   1

Chapter 2:

Destiny   7

Chapter 3:

A Friend   19

Chapter 4:

The Bad House, Part 1   33

Chapter 5:

The State of Jamanny   45

Chapter 6:

A Journey's End   75

Chapter 7:

The Rise of Dozer   79

Chapter 8:

The Bad House, Part 2   85

Chapter 9:

The Reunion   101

Chapter 10:

Faith's Revenge   109

Prelude

The purpled palms of a local undercover call girl, Mary Rae Anna, banged against the smooth wood surface of the locked bathroom door.

"When I get out of here, I'm going to kill you, you son of a bitch!" she screamed at the top of her lungs from behind a swollen blackened face and busted mouth. In hopes of knocking it down, she threw her full weight against the door; on the other side, the scarred, tall, wrinkled body of Jamanny Durgen calmly zipped up his soiled, insulated work suit.

Spitting teeth that Mary had previously knocked out into his freshly burnt hand, Jamanny dropped them into his pockets along with money from the woman's nearby purse. Snatching clean drapes from the windows, he wiped the blood from his clothes and dabbed at his scratched face. Having stealthily invaded her house and avoided any possible witnesses, Jamanny as if using Mary as a pawn in some sick game, had tricked her into having sex.

When he attacked her, he had found the big-boned, Caucasian woman's stubbornness and muscle quite hard to handle. With stab wounds on his legs and arms, he attempted to flee. Using a lighter, he lit a nearby candle and placed it in the oven. He twisted the dials on the gas stove to broil and the top burners to high and ran out of the house as fast as he could. "Another one bites the dust," He said.

He ripped off a fake banner from his old blue van, scanned the area, and smiled wickedly. Lighting a huge brown cigar, he left the premises trailing a cloud of awful smelling smoke.

Mary could not raise the used, worn-out pulley system on the heavy bathroom window high enough to escape. She caught the strong aroma of gas and screamed for help. Knowing the possibility of what could happen next, she took a few paces back. She took a deep breath and leaped off the edge of the tub. Without a second thought, she dove through the closed window and crashed to the snow-covered ground in an explosion of shattered glass and broken wood.

Shredded up and barely clothed, Mary rushed to the truck that she had slicked out of Joe, the neighborhood storeowner as her house exploded. Finding the extra set of keys under the floor mat, she started the car and glanced in fury at the dark pit of fire and smoke that rose from where her house had stood. Looking in the rearview mirror, she stared at her bruised and beaten face like a mad bull looking at a blotch of red.

"No, no, no! Manny ... you bastard ... you ... you—" she cried in anger and vengeance. Shifting to drive, she sped off after the man who had taken her lifestyle and altered her beauty.

Chapter 1:
FAITH

———— ✳ ————

As cold as it was, the sun still managed to shine more radiantly than it ever had. It was the brightest day of the entire winter. The bright sky was full of thick white clouds as if it was about to snow, but not one flake fell at this time.

Faith Hopkins, a young victim and survivor of rape and violence, stepped out of her front door and checked her mailbox in front of her apartment building. Covered in a warm, insulated leather coat with fur around its neck and sleeves, she carefully stepped around melted clumps of snow that had fallen the previous day. Creating a light crunching sound with the bottom of her boots as they touched down upon the surface, Faith clunked across the wooden deck, thinking only of the double funeral—for her mother and grandmother—that she was about to attend. A familiar blow from a car horn turned her head as she slid the key into the keyhole of the mailbox.

"All righty, come on, y'all!" she called to Richard.

He was an older man who had dated her mother; Faith considered him a stepfather. Destiny, her four-year-old daughter, stepped from behind him as they marched out of the apartment dressed in black.

"Well, we're ready." Richard locked the door and took Destiny's hand as her tiny black dress shoes tapped beneath her. "Are you ready, Destiny?" Destiny looked up at him and quietly shook her head. "Me either." Richard, suffering the terrible loss of his woman, pushed himself toward Faith and a large black hearse that waited by the curb.

1

The sound of the hearse's horn was just as Faith remembered it. It was the same as the one she had ridden in as a little girl during her father's funeral. Rekindling that same awful feeling of loss and hurt, she dabbed her eye with a balled up tissue. Not able to get through the tragedy by herself, Faith was happy to have true friends by her side.

Ousaynou, a close Senegalese male friend and Julia, her Caucasian best friend who had helped deliver her daughter, rode with her. The two were always there when she needed them and kept her company during the service. After sitting with her during the funeral ceremonies, they rode with her all the way to the graveyard as two officers on motorcycles led them to the burial site.

A funeral was already tough to deal with, but a double funeral was like dealing with a chainsaw to the heart. Faith managed to make it through. The unfortunate events that had led to the deaths of both of these women crippled the hearts and spirits of nearly every loved one left behind. Faith stood on the front lines of death and departure. Death was no longer a tale of her past but a cruel reality of the present. It still existed and would always continue to exist around her. The foul stain that it left behind within her now would carry on for the rest of her life, mentally and internally. Analyzing everything, she constantly sniffed into her saturated tissue. Dabbing at the corners of her eyes, Faith passed Richard two tissues, and he wiped his face clean of tears.

"Bleeding ulcers … internal bleeding? I can't believe I'm here and she's gone. We had just taken our last drink together … forever too. It was our last time. Who knew? She was so strong, even until her last. And her sweet old Momma!" Richard started to drift off. "She didn't even tell me that she was in pain until it was too—"

"Momma and Big Momma, they were both strong women, Richard." Faith tried to remember the good things about them.

Ousaynou gently pulled her close to console her. "Let's just pray and hope that the police do their part and find the person who started that fire."

The funeral was attended by a large number of relatives and friends. They slowly accumulated and gathered around the preacher as he spoke before the coffins were lowered. The wind blew gently against the remaining loose snow; it scattered about the ground like fine grains of sand on a paved beach walkway.

Faith watched her brother, Juni, make his second appearance since the viewing of the bodies. He hadn't been around anyone much, but—accompanied by a respectable young girl—he stood next to her in a suit and tie. Not wanting to stare, Faith turned away proudly. Seeing Richard and all the other people who had attended the burial of her two mothers made her smile and feel thankful for how blessed she was to have had both of them in her life.

Thinking of Big Momma's famous words, she repeated them in her mind. "Every queen has a princess, and every princess has to have faith, because in faith she will find her destiny." She recited the entire line over again to herself, pondering what her grandmother might really have been trying to say. "Every princess who has faith surely has a destiny to fulfill." She envisioned her mother answering her as she thought about her life, the world, and all of the struggling people in it. Glancing back toward the sky, Faith listened to the reverend finish his closing prayer.

"And as these two proud and strong women are laid in the final resting place, let us say our last good-byes here on earth and ask for GOD to open the gates of the heavens and let them enter that glorious place with him for the rest of their beautiful, spiritual lives. "Mrs. Queen (Big Momma) Thurgood and her loving daughter, Eunique (Princess) Hopkins, fine memories of the both of you will always be embedded in the hearts and souls of your family, friends, and loved ones forever. As the souls of your spirits leave us today in love and peace, we leave these old, used, and tired fleshy bodies behind in the darkness and cast them back into the earthly forms from which they came. Ashes to ashes, dust to dust, amen." The preacher gave family members and his men the signal to lower the coffins. Machines lowered the bodies of the mother and daughter into the cold ground.

A large percentage of the crowd broke into weeping, giving their last farewells. Faith stood silently, pouring tears, not quite able to shake the feeling of being responsible for their deaths. When Destiny ran up and squeezed her leg, Faith was instantly reminded why she had been given a second chance and who she needed to be strong for. Successful at raising her daughter and having survived one of the greatest tribulations of her life, a grateful feeling overcame her. She thanked her mother and grandmother again for everything they had done and for being in her corner when she had no one. Holding her head down toward her daughter, unknown members of her family encircled and embraced them with unimaginable, unconditional love. After the coffins reached the bottoms of the pits and the last flowers had been placed upon the foot of the plots, the crowd slowly dispersed.

Walking behind a line of her cousins, aunts, and uncles, Faith held Destiny's hand. Julia, Ousaynou, and Nodia—another sister-like friend who she grew up with—stepped along with her. Richard chatted with one of her grandmother's cousins, taking care of the arrangements for the hearse. Faith walked Ousaynou back to a rental car with her hand up under his left arm. Kashonda, another close friend from her childhood, waited in the driver's seat next to her trusty sidekick, Passion.

Overwhelmed by her thoughts, she listened to his words in one ear as her fingertips began to grow colder. Placing her hands in her coat pockets, Faith touched a sharp corner of her mother's obituary and pricked the soft meat under her fingernail. When she yanked her hand from her pocket, a small envelope sailed to the ground. Ousaynou picked up the letter and placed it in her hand.

Glancing at the IRS logo, she said, "My daddy hated them."

"Open it. It could be something good!" Julia said.

She unfolded the packet of stapled sheets of paper and began to skim through the small printed paragraphs. Jobless, she noticed her passing scores to the entrance exam at the bottom of the paper. Surprisingly, she was being offered a part-time position that could lead to permanent employment. Somewhat enlightened, she glanced at the shifts and times that she had to choose from. Shocked and slightly happy, she folded the papers into the envelope and placed them back in her pocket.

"Is everything all right?" Ousaynou asked with a strong hint of worry.

"Yes," Faith answered softly, nodding once.

"It's going to be all right." Ousaynou kissed her on the temple as she lifted Destiny into her arms.

Squeezed and leaned up against the skin of her mother's face, Destiny looked up into the sky. "Mommy?" She pointed above their heads.

Looking up, Faith could have sworn she had seen two angels floating toward her as the sensation of snow melted on the warm outer layer of her pupil. Suddenly, it flurried from the sky and over the close friends who loaded into Kashonda and Passion's rent-a-car. Thankful to still be able to be there for her child, Faith rode with her friends as they drove slowly back to her apartment.

Taking a deep breath and exhaling slowly, Faith held her daughter securely between her legs as they came to a smooth stop at a red light. Glancing over at her friends, she wiped her eyes as the streetlight sounded a quiet, high-pitched buzz. Proceeding forward, Faith caught a glimpse of an old man crossing the street. His cold, tired expression told a story of struggle and pain, giving her a small amount of inspiration. "Maybe the days ahead won't be as bad?"

Inside her heart, she felt that the worst was indeed behind her. Becoming a little more cheery, Faith took another deep breath and glanced out the window again. Patiently, she awaited the next tribulation that life had to offer. As they crossed the intersection, running a red light, horns blew at a blue van stopped directly in front of them in the middle of the street.

Aiming a semiautomatic handgun out the window, a scruffy, wrinkled, and sliced face stared directly into Faith's frightened eyes. Realizing what was going on, the entire car filled with screams, and a lone truck plowed through traffic from the opposite direction. From the other side of the van, Mary Rae headed for the vehicle at over ninety miles per hour.

Before Faith recognized Jamanny—her grandmother's old flame and the one she believed was solely responsible for her grandmother's death—a commotion in traffic caught his attention. Before he could pull the trigger, he turned around and abruptly shifted his car into reverse. He hit the gas just as Mary Rae's truck wrecked into the front of his van, ramming headfirst into Kashonda's small rental car. It flipped the automobile twice, ripping off a door, and sending Julia hurtling out of the passenger side. Somersaulting into traffic, the vehicle crunched over cars along the intersecting road and landed upside down. Skidding down the street, glass, plastic, and twisted scrap metal rained to the ground around the mangled automobile.

Faith, halfway out of the busted back window, opened her eyes and saw her hand mere inches from Destiny's left dress shoe. Her heart sounded as though it was pounding inside her brain. She attempted to scream to her daughter but was silenced by the puddle of blood that accumulated and gurgled inside her mouth.

During the darkest hour within the shadows of her deepest fear, she finally had become a faithful mother and a loyal servant of GOD and her own destiny. Dedicated to living and doing well for the future of her child, Faith remembered promising to be strong during the roughest of times. She had received a new beginning and a new meaning for life and her name. She awakened, reborn inside familiar flames of pain. Stretching down with her left hand, Faith felt for her child and Ousaynou, but her vision blurred and her heartbeat drastically declined. Taking hold of Ousaynou's cold hand, she remembered her last thoughts of marrying him. Then she had grim thoughts of him, perhaps he had been smashed to death inside the wreckage of the car.

Blacking out, Faith trembled, looking for warmth inside thoughts of Destiny, her mother, her father, and Big Momma. Picturing that beautiful smile for maybe the last time, she heard another familiar phrase from her grandmother.

"Every hummingbird catches the tune of the last."

A dark raspy voice laughed and softly whispered into the wind. Repeating the words from her trembling lips, Faith grazed Destiny's shoe with her fingertips and slowly closed her eyes at the sight of a silhouette of an old man carrying away the body of a little girl.

Chapter 2:
DESTINY

———— ✳ ————

All I ever wanted was a mother. All I ever wanted to be was a good daughter. I still love her, and I forgive her. She's still my mother, but I can hardly remember her face. She left me anyway. Why did she leave me in this place? I remember the breakfast and getting my hair done. There were other kids around too back then—and that old lady.

Nina dragged her feet slowly down the hall toward the open doorway. She twisted side to side in a small light blue dress, stained by play and a child's curiosity.

My mommy had a nice voice. Daddy says she left me with a friend in that car. That woman was stupid—all that smoke and fire. I can still remember her face. She looked mad and so sad.

Nina followed the dirty black lines that ran between the wooden floorboards with her eyes. Shuffling her fingers, Nina heard the laughter of an unknown voice ahead. One of her older brothers turned down the hall toward her with his new girlfriend.

"What are you doing down here? Get your tail upstairs—now!" Dozer pushed her to the floor in front of his doorway. His newfound love was an easygoing, skimpily dressed girl from outside. Opening his bedroom door, he mugged her into the room. "Get in there! She ain't my real sister." He slammed the door behind them.

Listening to the door lock, Nina pushed herself up from the floor and stood. When she walked into the next room, a clicking sound caught her attention.

Sitting in a rocking chair next to a small table, her father was taking a puff from his tar-stained tobacco pipe. Crossing one leg that seemed to stretch for miles from somewhere under the shadows of his stomach, Jamanny Durgen placed a lighter into the pocket of his shirt. As his tight, scruffy face and thick, graying eyebrows disappeared behind a newspaper, a thick cloud of smoke rose to the ceiling.

As Nina attempted to inch past without being detected, a great voice muttered her name, causing her legs to cease movement before the old man. Despite his odd behavior, she felt a slight gratitude toward him for being the only one in her corner.

"Tsk, tsk, tsk. Thinking again, are we?" The deep sounds from his vocal cords crept loudly from behind a spread of newspapers into her ears. "Now I done told you about traveling down here and wondering around—haven't I? You should be upstairs with the others at all times." Jamanny's last words repeated inside her mind like a skipping record.

"Everyone's mad at me; nobody likes me." Nina glanced at her feet. "I wish Mommy wouldn't have left us. I didn't even do anything." A tear trickled down her cheek.

"Your momma?" Jamanny said. "She left all of us for her own reasons, child! I gave her love, and she ran off and leaves me with you, your brothers, and sisters! I don't know why, but this was our destiny!" He laughed and sat the open newspaper on his lap. He smiled a rotten grin.

Breaking her sadness with a funny face, Jamanny smacked his large, dark lips and tilted his head. Placing a finger on one nostril, he leaned over and blew a slimy substance to the floor, close to the small child's foot.

Nina scrunched her face at the sight, and he pinched his nose clean and scratched an itch inside his ear with a large jiggling finger.

"You know … you are just as hardheaded as she was. Come!" He tossed the paper loosely onto the table. He aimed his discolored, gray eyes directly into her soul. "Your Mammy was a good woman, but sometimes she made the wrong choices. Remember when you were so mad at her that you tried to burn her house down? No? You don't really remember it? Humph, well, that's quite all right. You were just a baby in those days. You're so grown up now." He placed a trusting hand on the back of her neck and shoulders. "Say … what else do you remember?" He squeezed the back of her neck. "You can trust me."

Leaning into her, the old man made the little girl slightly uncomfortable. Trapped in uneasiness, Nina looked forward and said, "I just see fire and ..." She hesitated in the presence of his unmoved expression. "Fire and beans, that's all." Flashes of the tall man severely disciplining her siblings for little things convinced her to watch her tongue.

"Those are two things that you're gonna sure as hell remember—fire and beans." Jamanny laughed and lightly pressed against the tip of her nose. "Now are you absolutely sure that's all you remember? I mean, if you try really, really hard to think, is there anything else that you could possibly remember—that you would like to share with your good old Daddy?"

She closed her eyes tightly as if she was thinking hard and shook her head.

"Good." He raised a tall can of beer from beside his chair and pulled its aluminum key. Tilting the can away, he showered Nina with a short blast of fizzing foam and brew. "Yo Mammy left me with kids and you with an untrustworthy person who crashed a car with you in it. I brought you home with me so nobody could hurt you again! I loved that gal, but she was such a pussycat!"

Jamanny's thirteen-year-old orange cat, Tiger, jumped on the tabletop and nudged at his hand. Stroking the feline a few times, he put the cat on the floor and took a long hard swallow from the edge of the can, adding a lively belch. "You're growing up so damn fast and blossoming into such an alley cat yourself." He pointed a long finger and watched the cat go on about its way inside the house. "However, unfortunately for this case and pardon my French, but I am what they call a regular fuckin' junkyard dog around these parts. And you do by chance remember what dogs do to kitties?" He turned around to the table. Awaiting her answer, Jamanny slowly worked on finishing off the can.

Knowing that he didn't tolerate them using bad words, and not wanting to receive a beating, Nina pictured the time when her older sister responded to their father incorrectly. He had grabbed her by the neck and slung her across the room. Sensing that maybe she had ventured to the edge of crossing the line, her face drew long, and she said, "Dogs eat kittens."

"Exactly, ha, ha, ha! I guess what I'm really trying to say is that, one day soon, at a later time, you will sprout into a beautifully ripe alley cat. And because I am such a good dog, we will love each other, and the day will come when I will devour you. Not to fret, and don't you be scared because there is a moral to the story. Basically, we shouldn't let our memories turn us into a pussy before our time because, in the end, all we're going to do is get eaten." Jamanny sat back and winked, sending her heart racing into her stomach.

She remembered the sounds of him huffing and puffing behind the door of her sister's locked room. She snapped back to reality as her youngest sister, Pig, called her urgently from upstairs. Not knowing quite how to exit the room, she tried to ease away as a sick outburst of his laughter followed behind her.

Running into the displeased eyes of Miss Rashida, Jamanny's unclaimed, live-in girlfriend and caretaker of the house, Nina froze. Along with the other children, Nina always believed that Miss Rashida was their mother, but Jamanny always corrected the house with persistence when it drifted in that direction. She was always around when they needed her; the thirtyish woman stood in a flowery housecoat, pregnant again. She had been pregnant ever since Nina could remember.

Rashida glanced back at her through a pair of raccoon eyes. Rashida moved over to the sink as if she was in a trance. Nina had witnessed the woman's sanity slowly slip further and further away over time because of Jamanny's abuse.

"Woman!" Jamanny called from the other room.

"Coming," Rashida said with no emotion. She followed Nina with a lingering stare as she trotted toward the back hall that led upstairs. Lifting a coffee mug from the counter, she disappeared into the next room filled with Jamanny's yells and cursing. The intense commotion that repeated almost daily had stopped Nina once more inside the entranceway.

"Never tell him anything, especially things you remember." A familiar whisper tickled her ear, followed by a warm hand on her shoulder. "He hates that."

"He's always hitting her." Nina eased back into the hall next to her sister. Pig was just a few months older. The slapping sounds of her father's hand making contact with Rashida's soft skin were soon replaced by her crying. The coffee mug crashed to the floor and broke; the girls jumped back in fright. "I like her."

Nina's eyes began to water with every tug from her sister.

"Me too, come on."

Pig took Nina by the arm and dashed off quietly upstairs. Down the short stretch of hall, the pair turned left at Rashida's room. Taking a few steps, just ahead of them, Tina, the oldest of the daughters, ran out of the room, crying and holding her mouth. As they watched her storm across the hall into the playroom, her bedroom door swung open and slammed against the wall.

"What they doing down there?" Timothy, the teenage brother, stepped out into the hall, sweating and zipping up his pants. More noises came from downstairs. "Well—talk!"

"Fighting," Nina spit out. Pig quietly frowned like a guard dog behind her.

"What? Already? What's gotten into you two?" Timothy gallops off downstairs over-excited for no reason.

The playroom was a large room with a connecting bathroom at the left end, a hall in the middle, and the smaller kids' room on the right. The large room had dressers, a few broken toys, and a small coffee table in the middle of the floor. Nina and Pig heard small whimpers coming from their bedroom. Following the sounds, a dry, yellowish face smudged with dirt met them in the doorway.

"Why are you even talking to her?" Lamond, their seven-year-old brother, asked.

Omack, the baby boy, sat behind him on the bed.

Ignoring the comment, Pig shoved him aside and eyed her oldest sister curled up on the floor between the beds.

Even though Tina had been mean to Nina and her younger siblings, Nina still had a heart for her. She placed a gentle hand upon her big sister's deformed arm.

Pig knelt and softly rubbed her back. Tina sobbed against the floor under the bedroom window. Deep inside, Nina knew that whatever had happened wasn't her sister's fault. She used to believe that the creepy old house they lived in was the reason for bad things always happening. But the truth of the matter was that worst of all, their father's cold, bitter heart controlled everything.

Although he returned her home and continued to raise her, the older Nina grew, the more his way of living—and the story of how she came to be—made less and less sense to her. Having witnessed numerous accounts of violence and incest, she had become aware of the things that went on inside the house. The outcome of another episode had her reflecting on the tiresome tears of her older sister. Nina listened to Rashida's howls seeping hauntingly through the cracks of the floor. And as she helped console her sister and thought about her life, her future became clear. At the age of ten, Nina had determined that it was going to be hell living there—and hell getting out.

Squatting down, Nina wrapped her arm around her big sister. She and Pig reduced Tina's cries into a clash of sniffles. The horrible sounds continued to ring out from below. Used to being scared and abandoned, Nina couldn't help but think about the person who had left her.

Elsewhere, inside an old familiar place, memories of a lost child sustained life inside a paralyzed body. Inside a hospital room, a nurse recorded readings onto a chart, which was clipped against a folder on a clipboard. She placed it on the countertop while another trainee put away supplies. Pausing over the bed that belonged to a thin, lightly complexioned young woman with dreads, the trainee shook her head.

"I can't believe she's still here!" The trainee stored some extra gloves in one of the drawers on the front of the bed and placed a finger on its railing. "Sad. I hear they're planning on unplugging her soon—brain dead and no response. What a way to go. She's so pretty."

"I know, but check this out. Here's the weird part. They found her sitting up unconscious all by herself a few times. And once, they found her on the floor—like she'd just walked straight out of bed." The nurse moved next to the trainee. "Twitches too every now and then. Dr. Willis diagnosed it as some kind of unconscious nervous response. I don't know about that one, but that is why he gets paid the big bucks."

"Wow. That is wild. See, you have to watch these doctors too. Someone must really love her to keep holding on for so long."

"I'll tell you what. It's sad. I heard she was a sweet person. She must be loved because some rich lady's footing the bill. But it just goes to show you that, regardless of how sweet or nice you are, when your time's up, your time is up. It's a shame because she lost her grandmother and her daughter."

"How do you know so much about her?" The trainee brushed the patient's locks with her hand.

Looking in both directions, the nurse glanced at her co-worker. "Because Nurse Julia was her best friend, and she used to watch her daughter, Destiny." She gave the signal to leave.

"Poor Julia and Destiny." The trainee sighed before they left the room.

And as they left, their conversation sparked a chain reaction of emotions and mixed memories within the shell of the seemingly lifeless body of Faith Hopkins. But mainly it was the name—the last word spoken by the nurse—that disturbed her sleeping, nearly dead soul.

The sound of her daughter's name, Destiny, echoed inside her. Memories of holding the precious child for the first time fueled a reaction of electrical movement throughout her nerves. Visions of being with her little girl in the park and other memorable moments warmed Faith's heart with joy—until the tragic scenery of Destiny passed out in her arms inside the burning house sent the mighty muscle racing deep inside her chest.

Tears trickled and her blood began to pump as Faith's body jumped and jerked to the turning of dreams toward the dark side of her life. Forced to revisit the violent means of how she became impregnated, Faith experienced the rape again, and the images nearly took her breath away. Suddenly, in a cold stare at his burnt and bloody face, his head exploded, revealing her grandmother behind him, holding a smoking shotgun.

Consumed in fire and smoke, the old woman fell as flashes of a white woman transformed into the silhouette of the old man carrying away her daughter. The tall man turned to her as she made him out to be the father of her attacker.

"Jamanny Durgen," Faith whispered as her wide oval eyes opened, and her teeth clenched down on something cold between them. Feeling a sudden harsh burning in her chest, she reached out, grabbed a cord in front of her, and pulled out the long, slender breathing tube from her esophagus. Gagging and choking, she breathed in new life as she thought of murdering the man who was responsible for taking everything from her.

Fueled with fire, her fist clamped tightly with energy as she sat up in the bed, stretching free of the IV tube in her arm. Coming to, her eyes began to slowly focus on the dim lights that flickered and blinked on the medical devices next to the bed. As the conversation from the two nurses dissipated down the hall, it also indicated that she was in a hospital. Glimpsing around the dark room, Faith spotted a medical file on a counter below a small row of medical cabinets.

Recalling the vocals of the two women, she knew that—despite how much time had passed and regardless of how many police were on the case—apparently her daughter was still nowhere to be found. Faith knew exactly who had taken her. A strong, painful gut feeling lingered and ached inside. It told an unwanted truth of the great possibility that her only child was already dead. Memories of her hellish past flickered inside her head as she debated between waiting for a doctor and waging revenge on her family's true killer.

The justice system was slow, unreliable, and unpredictable. In Faith's current state of mind, if she went after the old man, she was determined not to come back alive without her daughter. All her life, she had done the right things and tried to make the best decisions despite the terrible things that she had been through.

Her hand slowly moved over the buzzer to the room's intercom. Eyeing the door, all the wires attached to her, and the monitors displaying her vital signs, she knew that if she unattached the diagnostic machines, they would sound an alarm. It would sound as if someone's heart had failed, summoning nearby doctors.

"Who am I kidding?" she muttered in sadness.

Hurt, overwhelmed, and tired of the position of being tragedy's pawn, she thought of tasty revenge. However, the idea of dying from going after someone singlehandedly—even though she wasn't a killer or a fighter—felt slightly silly and unwise.

"I'm a nice girl." Smirking foolishly in the dark room, she softly wiped the tears from her face. Taking a deep breath, she exhaled and lowered the call button, which was actually the remote to the television that hung from the ceiling. She envisioned the double funeral, burying her two mothers. Inside she heard a loud crash and red smoke looming around her. In her thoughts, she could vividly see the old man carrying off her child.

For a moment, as the night nurses and hospital staff went about their duties, the floor grew tolerably calm and quiet. A loud buzz and flashing red lights indicated that someone had flat-lined in room 36. Rushing into the room, the nurses instantly discovered that the body of their comatose patient, Faith Hopkins, was missing. Notifying the doctors, security, and proper authorities, the staff scrambled to find her.

Down the maze of hallways, a couple slept in a small, empty lobby. They were cuddled under a blanket; their loved one's bag of extra clothes was missing. And through the endless floors, some empty and some barely occupied, Faith left the hospital, dashing into the parking lot. Stumbling to the ground, she crawled close to the large rear tire of a car, just able to see the smokers and witnesses pointing out to security the direction that they thought she had gone.

As they proceeded to search the grounds, trembling and tired, Faith stayed low inside the large half-occupied parking lot. Soon she found her way into the nearby woods. Driven solely by the thoughts of her daughter, Faith pushed to the outskirts of a local park and fell between some bushes and the trunk of a large tree. "Protect me, FATHER. Give me strength," Faith prayed wearily, head down in the mud and dirt.

Out of breath and energy, she rolled on her back and stared at the sky. Exhausted, her heavy eyelids closed and the stars faded into black as she dozed off under the haze of the moon.

The hours that passed were kept warm by Faith's own demons. Restlessly combating in her sleep, she awakened to the view of a man crouching over her, squeezing her breast. As he reached out to touch her face, Faith's teeth crunched down on three of his fingers.

"Ow, you little filthy bitch!" A homeless man in ripped jeans and an old T-shirt snatched his burning hand out of her mouth. His red stubbly face smelled of cheap liquor as he wrapped his hand in a handkerchief. "I was just trying to help, you whore! This'll teach you!"

He smacked her back into the damp earth.

Jamming her foot into his crotch, Faith punched him in the mouth, bending two teeth back. A silver filling spun wildly into the air. As the man took his turn on the ground, Faith stood over his subdued body.

"This time, you live. Next time, you won't live long enough to swallow another sip. No one touches me without consent." She looked down at his feet before glancing at hers. Sizing them up, she pulled the man's boots off of his feet and put them on. "You got girl feet."

She grinned wickedly while eyeing a small paper bag in his possession.

"You taking my shoes and what? Now you think you're gonna steal my food too? Fuck you. Wait till I get up! I'm a fix you real good, you hooker!"

The man wheezed, slowly rising to a sitting position as his angry stare found Faith's cold, emotional eyes.

"Aw nuts." Faith stomped between his legs a few more times to ensure her safety—and that the stranger wouldn't get up anytime soon. As blood stuck to the heel of her boot, the man's mixed cries of pain and agony carried through the emptiness of the park. The familiar pitch of the poor fellow's voice reminded her of the shrill that emitted from the smoking body of her former attacker and ex-boyfriend, Jamondo, on the floor of her grandmother's burning house.

Suspiciously looking around, she snatched the small paper bag from the quivering hands of the man. "Give me the goddamn hamburger!" Faith opened the brown greasy bag. Half starving, she walked away, gorging on the two cold cheeseburgers.

With nowhere to go and no one to turn too, Faith found herself sitting alone on a bench, starring through passing traffic at some place beyond the middle of the street. With portions of her memory still missing, she rubbed both sides of her temples and considered how to get on the trail of Jamanny.

Unable to remember friends or put names with faces, flashes of the hospital's ceiling lights and the mixed sounds of distinct voices rambled through her brain. Out of all that she could recollect, only the recent sounds of bits and pieces of the nurses' conversation stuck out like a sore thumb in her mind. "Brain dead and no response, some … rich lady's footing the bill."

She sat upright, lifted up her shirt, and pulled out the manila folder that she had swiped from the hospital. Opening the folder, Faith skimmed through it intensely, immediately coming to a name: Mary Rae Anna. Signed mainly as the consent signature and several times too many, the name raised a red flag in Faith's brain. She began to picture a wild-haired Caucasian woman and seeing her in scenes throughout her life. Identifying her as being the levelheaded, sassy best friend of her mother, she also recalled the woman was not only sweet, but she was secretly an undercover hooker.

Faith's blood pressure began to rise again as she remembered how her daughter ended up in the care of Mary Rae Anna. Having come for her child, Faith found the woman having sex with Jamanny for money. Who knew that face and those eyes would be embedded in her brain forever just like those of her attacker?

Picturing the double funeral and the car crash, she remembered seeing the woman inside the car that she had collided with—along with Jamanny carrying away her child. Since Mary Rae Anna had been known for having clients, there was a good chance that she still had contacts with the old man. Faith wondered what had happened between them. Why had the woman paid to keep her alive all this time? Perhaps it was out of remorse—or maybe the two were conspiring together in some sort of elaborate scheme. Whatever the case, the situation churned inside her in anger and fire.

Chapter 3:
A FRIEND

———— ✻ ————

The thirst for vengeance gradually descended from the gloom that covered the world that Faith remembered. She transformed into something else by night: a carefree, coldhearted, lone warrior. For the next thirty-six hours, Faith harassed single women, stalked old ladies, scared little girls, and snatched blond wigs off of men. Since the victims were all Caucasians, her acts started to appear racist.

The process of seeking out every Mary Rae Anna in the phonebook with aggression finally got her to the bottom of the telephone listing. Desperate, but with no leads to her daughter, Faith ended her journey in front of an establishment with the name Mary Rae's Palace in bold flashing letters upon its roof. By the types of people who were standing in front and coming in and out of the building, Faith sensed that this was some sort of upscale escort service or swingers club. Small parties of drunks, half-drunken couples, and trios exited the building in sexy smiles combined with fancy attire. As they entered limos and classic rides, Faith, covered in dirt and sweat, dragged her tired body past the parking attendants and up the concrete stairs toward the entrance. With fierce determination to find this woman from her nightmarish memories, Faith stormed through the double doors with her adrenaline pumping.

A large hall decorated with elegant chandeliers and doors stretched around Faith. There was a desk and an elevator at the far end. Slowly and silently, she walked to the desk. A tall, slender man dressed as a waiter or servant looked her up and down disgustingly before disappearing into a room full of loud, diverse socializing. Under a low violin playing over an intercom, a large, distinctive man sat next to a devious brunette at a cherry oak desk. She was wearing ten coats of glossy, red lipstick. Ceasing their intense conversation upon eyeing the savage looking woman, the man's mouth dropped open as the woman's unnerving gum popping popped one last time.

"Uh, can we help you?" the woman said from under her bangs. As Faith slowly approached, the woman looked over at the man. "Okay."

"I think we got a live one," the man whispered across the table. "Here we go." He loosened his collar and stood up. "Can we help you?"

Nearing the table, Faith cracked her neck twice. Clothed in mud, with a stick tucked in the front of her pants, Faith stood before them, staring blankly. Rolling her tongue against her tartar-encrusted teeth, Faith tilted her head and turned her attention to the man. "I'm a friend of Mary Rae Anna. I'm here to see her."

"Mary Rae Anna? Is she talking about Mary Rae, the owner?" The man rubbed his head and snickered to his co-worker.

"No one sees her. Don't you have a direct line, Mary Rae Anna's friend?" The woman sat upright and stared into Faith's thirsty glare.

Glancing back and forth between the two, Faith's pupils fixed with focus. "It's important. She owes me a favor." Her dreads fell beside her face as she lowered her head and tightened her fist.

"Wait. Is she serious? Let me see. You march in here with no appointment, looking like anything, tracking dirt all over the floor— and GOD knows what else! And on top of that, you come in demanding to see the owner?"

The man moved to escort the crazed woman off the property.

"I'm sorry but, we can't let you go up." The woman crossed a leg, leaned back confidently, and watched the man reach out for Faith's arm.

Within minutes, inside the president of the company's personal office, a large woman unplugged the phone that continuously rung, to rest her mind and eyes from hours of making irritating phone calls and completing heaps of paperwork. Her teased red hair bounced side to side, and with her mouth cocked open, she imagined the words: "Kick it open!" Her office door burst open and slammed against the wall. Popping up in her seat, she sent a stack of organized papers helicoptering to the floor. The brunette woman from the front desk appeared in the office as the silhouette of another stood halfway in the doorway.

"Mary, Mary Rae? We tried to call you. I'm so sorry! It's this crazy woman." Sporting a freshly bruised left eye, the desk woman trembled in front of the startled woman.

"Shut that shit up! Is she in there? Move your ass—unless you want some more!" Faith yelled.

Eyeing Mary Rae Anna with an attitude, the desk woman moved from in front of the desk, holding her bleeding mouth, and whispered, "She's a lunatic! She's got Dave!"

"Wait, wait! Slow down. Ow! What else do you freakin' want? I don't get paid enough for this, Mary Rae! We brought you to her!"

Dave entered the room bent completely over with Faith holding one arm behind his back. The pointy end of a plunger handle was jammed through his pants and into his rectum. "This ain't good, Mary!" He screamed in pain as Faith stood behind him, locked on Mary's pale, shocked face.

Flashes of times around Mary Rae Anna entered Faith's mind when she looked at her. Scenes of Mary with her daughter, mother, grandmother, and Jamanny inflamed her rage. "Where's that fuckin' monster and my daughter, bitch?" Faith applied pressure to the stick. As the man attempted to collapse to his knees in screams and tears, Faith forced him to continue to stand. "Where's my baby?" she yelled as people from around the building began to gather in the halls outside the room.

"Holy horseshit!" Mary said. "You're here. Let him go, Faith. How did you get out the hospital? Why didn't anyone call?" It slowly registered that she had unplugged the phone.

"Mary, I'm calling the police!" an employee hollered from the doorway.

"No, it's okay! Get out of here!" Mary said, waving the man off with a handful of rings. "It's going to be okay." She took a deep, hard swallow. "It's been seven whole years, Faith, and I've just spent the last three days cursing the hospital to hell looking for you. Now, we need to talk—woman to woman." She tugged on her red suit dress. One arched brow curled like a sailor, and a drawn mole kept her crooked mouth sexy. "Things from this point on aren't going to get any easier, sweetie. Faith, please, for the love of GOD, let that man go. He's a good man. He doesn't have anything to do with this. This is between me and you."

She grinned crookedly. Wrinkling her forehead, she looked serious and trustworthy. Sliding her long painted nails down her large thighs to the open slit of her dress, Mary Rae Anna cracked open the third drawer just below her knee, positioning her hand by her gun.

Holding her ground for a moment, Faith released her grip on the plunger. Stepping to the side, she allowed two men from Mary Rae's staff to assist their injured friend.

"That a girl." Mary Rae Anna sat back and sighed in relief. "Turner, get Dave to the doctor like yesterday, please! Lacy, clear the halls and get someone to fix this door. Let's get this under wraps—and I want this kept on the hush! And let's get some ice on that mouth. I'm going to take care of you guys. I promise! Sorry about this, guys, but she's like family."

As everyone exited the room and hall, Faith snatched the plunger out of the man's behind and tossed it into the garbage can next to the door.

"Faith!" Mary shook her head.

The injured desk man screamed, "I'm going to sue you!"

"Oh my goodness. Faith, you really shouldn't have done that." She imagined all the negative attention and court dates that were going to be a result from the incident.

"Where's my baby, Mary?" Faith gazed deeply into her eyes like a hungry tiger waiting for meat.

Mary Rae Anna rolled from around her desk in a wheelchair. "It's been a long time, Faith. Your mom—"

A swift slap pushed her deep into the cushion of her seat before she could even begin.

"Don't you dare bring my mother up! You betrayed us. We let you into our family, bitch, and you were fucking that animal the entire time that he was plotting to kill us!" Faith pointed and waved her finger in the woman's face. "The three people who I love the most aren't here with me. For all I know, you could have helped in conspiring your little bed buddy's game. Now, I'm going to ask this one more time, and if I don't receive an honest, fitting answer, I'm going to kill you and hurt as many people as I can. I'm burning this goddamn building to the ground! Where is my baby—and where is that little thing of a creature you let between your legs?"

Realizing that she was dealing with a ticking time bomb, Mary Rae Anna wiped the corner of her mouth and checked her hand for any sight of blood. Sniggering to herself, Mary Rae sat up and lit a cig. "I'll tell you what, little lady. I'll admit that I might have deserved that, but I do declare that's going to be the last slap that this old coon is taking. You pack a punch!" She wiggled her chin with one hand. "Faith, look. I don't know about half the things coming out of your mouth, and I'm truly sorry for what's happened to you. But, whatever part that you think I play in all of this just isn't true. It isn't like that at all. I want that bastard dead—just as much as you do." Her large bedroom eyes began to water.

"I'm all ears." Faith was preparing to react at the first detection of a lie.

"Look at me. Look at my eyes." Mary Rae braced one hand on the armrest and leaned forward. "Your mother was like a real good friend and the closest thing that I've had to a sister. When my own family turned their backs on me, she was the only person on the planet that was there for me, and I will always be in debt to her. I know we have had our differences, but you're like a niece to me—my only one. I would never purposely do anything to hurt you, your daughter, or your mom. That's why I did everything in my power to keep you alive, including changing my life. I owe you and your mother. That's why I held on, Faith, to keep you alive! I damn near went broke saving you!" Her face turned red as tears rolled down her cheeks.

"Then why were you with Jamanny? Why did you crash into our car after the funeral—just before he kidnapped my daughter?" Faith's emotions began to get the best of her. "It's the second time I remember you two being in the same place at the same time! How could you have a relationship with him—my grandmother's ex?"

"A relationship? What? There wasn't one! Faith, back then, I was wild, stupid, and desperate for money. I did anything for the mighty dollar, including selling my own body. All of that talk I did and that act I put on about being a lady—hell, I was a prostitute! Your mother knew, but she never judged me. She helped me to keep it semi-safe and, eventually, I learned a better method. Now I have priorities. Before, I was a lady—now I'm a woman. I thought Jamanny was the best quick way to get on top. I never knew that he was Big Momma's ex. I just thought he was an old man with money. And you know what, after that first time he saw you, he did make little comments after that—like he knew you—now that I think about it. But I cursed him out every time. I should have paid more attention, but I just never went there with him—and never asked questions. I didn't have time to get to know them; it was all about sex and money." She pulled a small glass from the inside of her suit jacket. Sliding two fingers inside her large curled hair, she pulled out a tiny bottle of liquor and emptied it into her shot glass. "On the day of the funeral, he hurt me real bad—nearly beating the crap out of me. I tried to kill him, but it backfired and I nearly killed—"

Her plump hands began to shake, covering the tears dripping down across her palms.

"I didn't know that you were in that car. I didn't find out until afterward. I felt terrible. I got depressed. I didn't know what to do. He took my whole world."

Faith was listening somewhere behind a dark grim stare.

"I used every inch of brain and energy I had to save you. It was the least I could do. I owe you. I hired every gangster and two-bit criminal that I could to find and kill him for what he did to me." She took the shot glass and threw it back. "Nobody's found him—nobody's heard of him. It's like he vanished off the face of the goddamn earth." Mary Rae Anna took another puff off her cigarette and put it out, noticing the thick silence that filled the room. "What I don't get is why you think he wants Destiny. And what do you mean when you said he plotted to kill you? What happened? Faith, what did that son of a bitch do to you?" Her nose flared and her blue eyes became sharp at the mere idea of Jamanny harming Faith or her family.

Determining that out of all they had experienced with each other, maybe there was the odd possibility that Mary Rae Anna was still her mother's best friend—the same sweet, caring, spirited person Faith had always known.

In a silent stance of flowing tears, Faith tilted her head back and closed her eyes. Since she had no help and no leads, she knew that eventually she would have to trust and confide in someone. She took a deep breath and said, "Jamanny ... was originally my grandmother's, well, Big Momma's old boyfriend. He was a happy farmer once, with land and a decent life, until some people came and took it away. Then things changed. He started drinking, cheating, lying, and putting his hands on my grand-momma, forcing her to leave just to get away from him. One night, after she left him, while she was asleep, he gouged out her eye and tried to kill her. But she ran him off and shot him in the shoulder. He was never seen again—or so she thought. The truth of the matter was that he secretly watched her and stalked her for years. He followed her and watched her kids and grandkids grow into adults as often as he wanted too. He and one of his sons had this weird thing with this crazy woman too. They both had children by her—under the same roof. In revenge toward Big Momma, he raised ... I think ... and sent his son to come after me and rape me. Since I never got a look at his face, later in life, he befriended me and tried to kill all of us."

"What, that crazy bird who you were dating? What was his name—Mondo? I should have known. I don't believe this mess; that's insane! He was Jamanny's son?"

Mary tried to absorb it all at once.

"Come to find out that his name wasn't Mondo; it was Jamondo Durgen—the son of Jamanny Durgen. Anyway, he followed me to Big Momma's house, and she killed him before she passed. While we were fighting, he set the house on fire with us in it. The ceiling caved in on Big Momma—that's what killed her. When I escaped, I saw Jamanny running with a container of gas in his hand. And that was the day I realized that I had been seeing him throughout my whole entire life. I just didn't know who he was. He'd been around all that time, probably murdered some of our other relatives—and we didn't even know. He had this old van that I recall seeing. He must've painted it or changed the outside signs on it all the time. I just remember seeing him and this van parked everywhere. He's been waiting to get back at my grandma." Faith stepped back and leaned against the wall. "And he did."

"And I was just a pawn in his game too—an easy piece of ass to him. I hope he got a piece of a sour pussycat. How's about them apples?"

Mary rubbed her head and blew into a tissue. Squeezing the top of her nose, she relieved her sinus pressure. "I have rooms here, and you're more than welcome to stay as long as you need. I guess I should call the hospital and—"

"No!" Faith said. "Maybe it's best that I remain missing for right now."

"Remain missing? Faith, what? What if you're sick? Who do you think you are—a secret agent or something? Faith, think about—"

"Mary Rae, no! Please? I have to find out what happened to my daughter. All my life, Jamanny has had me and my family in his radar. Maybe it's time for me to be invisible for a change. It's time to hunt for the hunter."

Despite the darkness, Faith looked down at Mary Rae Anna with a glowing aura of hope and strength.

"Ladybug, you have woken up into a grown Rambo, bitch! I don't believe this, but I like it."

Mary flipped a strand of hair and laughed as Faith tilted her head and cracked a small smile.

With the same common enemy, Faith figured that she could trust the woman who she had once thought of as an aunt. Feeling slightly better, she took a seat in a small chair against the wall. Regrouping her thoughts and energy, she talked, listened, and watched Mary Rae Anna plug in her phone and make calls to silence the events that had occurred. Waiting while the woman got her squared away, Faith couldn't help but think about her mother, to whom she had never gotten the chance to say her last good-byes. Interrupted by scenes of her grandmother saving her, a vision of little Destiny ended the mournful memories, sending Faith sobbing against the wall.

The following morning, inside one of the more lavish suites, establishment, Mary Rae Anna found Faith doing push-ups on the floor. "Hot damn girl, you're gonna bust a fuse before your engine even starts!" She stopped her automatic wheelchair and sipped a mug of hot coffee. "You just came back from the dead, and now you're training to be a soldier?"

"Mary," Faith said as she slowly got up and sat on the bed. "What exactly is this place?"

"This, my little china doll, is my baby, Mary Rae's empire!" Mary Rae rolled her chair over to the window and opened the blinds. "I went from hooker to Boss Madame in a matter of two years. I'm not afraid to admit it. It was my choice, my life. This is my enterprise, my own private club, pub, escort, dating service, mini hotel, and banquet hall all rolled into one. I provide high-end rooms and service to these high rollers out here in the world. In return, they pay me a pretty penny. It's all legal, and no sex is involved from me. Average Joe's don't get in her either. The rooms are usually empty, but when I get a bite, man it's something." She peered out the window at the clear sky. "I had to try to save you. I had to do something; that darn hospital was so expensive."

Faith could feel the sincerity and love radiating from Mary's soul. The time when she had strutted around glamorously suddenly came to mind. Paralyzed from the car incident, it was an amazing feat that she had achieved this level of success from a wheelchair. And even more touching was that her drive was Faith and her family.

"Thank you, Mary. Sorry for the mess I made here last night—and for putting my hands on you."

"It's quite all right, Faith. I understand. I know you didn't mean it. Heck, I would have walked in here the same way if I was wearing your shoes. I'm just happy you found me." Mary Rae Anna pulled out a red eyeglass case from her bra. Taking out her thin specs, she blew hot air onto the lens, wiped them, and softly placed them upon her face. Turning her chair, she moved over to the bed and nudged Faith's chin gently up. Seeing her pain, sadness engulfed Mary's heart even more. "What are you thinking? What are we going to do?"

Taught to fight and never give up, Faith thought of her vow to protect her daughter. Having witnessed the deaths of her loved ones—and having nearly lost Destiny several times—she turned away and hit the palm of her hand. "I'm going to find Jamanny," she said.

She placed all her sadness in a box and left it behind, buried in hell and anger. Pushing her focus, she was determined to find out what had happened to her child and devoted her time to retracing her steps. Gaining access to the Internet, she searched for clues and dug for information at the public library. She learned that her old apartment was occupied by a new family. She tried again the next day and the day after, searching onward.

It wasn't until the night of a full moon that Faith received her first lead. The quietness of the old neighborhood was broken by the sound of falling glass shattering across a floor and the squeaks of a screen door unlocking. Inside the tattered old house where Faith had learned the truth about her boyfriend, she slid her hand through the window of the back door that she had thrown a brick through earlier that day.

Unlocking the top latch, she floated inside and softly closed the door. Clicking a small flashlight, she held it low, illuminating the small portion of the floor in front of her. Stepping out of a small hall, she entered the kitchen. Dirty dishes and trash covered the countertops and oak table. She stopped and peered into the dust and cobwebs.

In the adjoining living room, chills glided down her skin, along with a sensation of vulnerability. The memory of Rashida Harrison, the crazed lover of Jamanny and his son, haunted her in every brush against the old furniture. Clear of most of the clutter that had occupied the house, the living room echoed with traces of children and life. Walking past the old torn couches that hid under a collection of filth and litter, Faith checked for anything of use.

Stumbling upon a familiar fold-out chair on the coffee table, Faith pictured the deranged woman cursing in an uproar while slicing her arm violently with a butcher knife. Wads of articles and newspapers crunched under her feet. Glimpsing two empty shelves, she high-stepped over a pile of old clothes to an intersection of rooms.

She remembered Rashida's children laughing and chattering as she opened a door that led to the next floor. She checked the remaining rooms on the floor; the top level revealed nothing of significance either. She checked the children's rooms and what she thought was the adult room one last time. With not much to go through, Faith stood in the middle of a large queen-sized bed frame. Ready to quit, she placed her hands on her hips and thought hard and fast.

Coming up with nothing, Faith turned off the flashlight and walked over to the window. The stars twinkled against the infinite blue sky while a police car patrolled the street. A bright spotlight flashed in the house; Faith leaped to the side of the windowsill. *I definitely don't need this.*

Bad feelings sunk over her shoulders and into her stomach. With her heart racing in her chest, Faith waited as the police cruiser slowly continued down the street. Deciding it was a sign to leave, her flashlight dropped to the floor and turned on. Picking it up, she unearthed the tip of a yellow piece of paper. Squatting, she grinned deviously. She blew the dust off an old receipt and stood. *Gotcha!*

The following day, Mary Rae Anna escorted her to the sacred grounds where Big Momma's house had stood. Within the burnt and black outlines of the house, beams and fallen frames hid inside shrubbery, grass, and wooden boards. A butterfly fluttered softly along the cat legs of the upstairs tub that protruded, upside down, halfway out of some sort of black mound of burnt material. Tiny insects took shelter inside a portion of the kitchen that was still standing; the back of a couch seemed to crawl from the earth. As Faith touched it, a ladybug fled into the air, reminding her of how peaceful her grandmother's house had been. "I can't believe it's all gone," she said.

"Life is funny like that sometimes, hun," Mary Rae Anna said. "Things happen to everybody and to the best of us. Occasionally, it has a tendency to give us not what we want, but what we need, whether we like it or not. But what can we do about it?"

Faith was staring at a woman holding flowers across the lot.

"Who is that? She looks familiar." Faith stared even harder, trying to identify her. As the woman tossed the flowers to the ground, she looked up and stared at Faith.

"I can't see that far with these old eyes," Mary said with a laugh. "Sounds like you're regaining some memory—good."

"Faith? Faith?" Slowly walking toward her, the Caucasian woman's smile grew with every step.

Moments after giving birth and other occasions of being in the woman's presence shot through Faith's mind. The face came to her as belonging to someone that had been close to her.

"What? I don't believe it! Faith? It is you!" The woman walked up and hugged her. "When did you get out the hospital?" She looked over at Mary Rae Anna in the wheelchair. "Hello, Mary. You never returned my calls. I left a hundred messages. You could have told me she was out!"

Mary Rae Anna just shrugged.

"You look so familiar." Faith peered into her bright eyes.

"Familiar? You're joking? She's kidding me, right?" The blonde woman glanced back and forth at them, realizing that Faith was serious. "Faith, it's me, Julia, your best friend. The one who helped deliver your daughter." Julia pushed her sunglasses on top of her head and looked Faith in the eyes.

"She's suffering from a slight memory loss. It's gonna take her some time to catch up," Mary said.

"Julia … I do know you." Faith's eyes begin to tear as flashbacks of the times spent with her whipped through her brain. "Sorry. I just couldn't remember your name. Jay!"

"It's been a long time, girl. How long have you been out the hospital?"

"Weeks. What are you doing here?"

"Something told me to come out and pay respect to your grandmother. Look at who I run into? I liked her a lot. Her house was always so peaceful. She was like a grandmother to me too."

"I don't remember too much of her—only the bad stuff. I guess I don't recall too much of anything really."

"No friends? No relatives? Remember Ousaynou? He's an officer now. He's been waiting on you to wake up. So what about—"

"No." Faith cut her off before she could even bring up her daughter's name. "I don't really have time for friends right now. My daughter is still missing."

"What, still? Aw, Faith, I'm sorry. If there's anything I can do to help, let me know. I don't have a life or job at the moment. I'm pretty much free anytime. Man, that ticks me off, it makes you want to go out and kill somebody! I love that little girl. Excuse me." Julia, red in the face, stepped away to blow her running nose and to wipe her tears.

The plush head of a pony poked out of the dirt and caught Faith's attention. She dusted off the toy and placed it under her arm. "Mary?"

"Yes, doll?" Mary Rae Anna adjusted her sunglasses and looked back at the driver who waited next to her limo.

"I'm going to be leaving soon. I'm going to need one last favor from you."

"What? So soon? Faith, have you thought about this? You only got out the hospital two weeks ago." Mary Rae was stunned by what she was hearing. "I think eventually the police will turn up something, Faith—if we wait."

"Mary!" Faith said. "I think I've found him. I came across a moving truck receipt yesterday. I went to the moving company and got information on where they went. It's not exact, but it's close. I have to check it out." She caught a glimpse of Julia, looking at her in disbelief, in the reflection of Mary's sunglasses. "Alone."

"Why can't I go with you—or send some of my people with you? Could be a ghost mission? Some police manpower wouldn't hurt either!" Mary Rae Anna was worried about Faith.

"Faith, I know I just came back into your life, but maybe you should listen to her?" Julia, having overheard the conversation, couldn't hold back any longer. "That's crazy and suicidal—you could die!"

"No, I want to make sure it's him. I can't afford anything going wrong—or anyone else getting hurt. I have to do this alone. I will get my daughter—or at least find out what happened to her. It's my destiny."

"Faith, no. Don't do this. I just found you! You're going to get yourself killed!" Julia said.

Faith said, "It's going to be okay."

"No, it's not. Oh my goodness. I'm not going to stand by and let you do something stupid! Apparently she's been listening to you because she's here! What have you been telling her?"

Mary Rae Anna rolled her eyes and shook her head.

"Why don't you say something to stop her? Faith, you just said that you don't have anyone. Well I'm here. I found you! You're all I had, Faith. Believe it or not—your family was my family."

"Julia, listen. This is not about you, and this is not about me. This is about my daughter and her life. Time has already gone by—chances are good that she's already dead! I need to know what happened! The police haven't found her, and no one can help me but GOD. I'm sorry, but I'm not the same person you think I am. I have to do this. Mary, thank you for everything, but I need two things from you."

"Anything, Faith. What is it?" Mary tossed the roses onto the ground. "If anything was to ever happen to you, I'd never forgive myself."

"Some cash and a set of wheels." Faith released three white roses as Mary and Julia looked at each other.

Chapter 4:
THE BAD HOUSE, PART 1

———————— ✳ ————————

A canine growled and snarled as a sudden repeating yelp swept past light fixtures and crumbling paint, traveling between the cracks and holes in the upstairs floorboards of an unknown house deep inside the boonies of Mississippi. Triggering the smallest of the children to run curiously toward the sound, the emotion led them to the living room of Jamanny's estate.

Under the dim lights, Jamanny worked out both arms with a pair of dumbbells. Looking down at his veiny arms, he dropped the iron weights on the floor and retrieved a small pill bottle from his shirt pocket. Taking off his unwashed ball cap with a faded logo on the front, Jamanny wiped his balding head and gently placed the cap on the table.

Under his thick gray brows, his glassy eyes gazed above a twitching nose. Crinkled lips tightened as if he'd left a finger plugged into an electrical socket; white hair stood wildly on his head.

"Pumpkin? You know Tiger is enough, and you all don't want to clean after him! I do it!" His deep voice crackled from his dry throat. "When I asked you the other day if you had brought some sort of animal into my home, what did you tell me, pussycat? How did you answer?" He took another whiff of the aroma that floated about the musty house.

"No." Nina stood, covering her face. Turning, she saw the stray puppy that she had snuck into the house. It was crippled, having barely survived her father's unpleasant kick.

"Now Nina ..." Jamanny paused, lifting a dumbbell. "Can you explain to me then, why I'm knee deep in dog shit inside my own goddamn home?" he yelled at the top of his lungs.

Invisible inside his massive free hand, the lid of the pill bottle shot onto the floor with the flick of his large thumb. As the oldest of the children joined the others, he popped an unsafe dosage of steroids into his mouth. Stuffing the tablets between his tongue and teeth, he swallowed them whole without liquid. Impatiently he waited for a response from the frail child, but she just stood there in tears. "Answer me! You're not going to say nothing?" He launched the dumbbell into the air, spinning just past her face, in the direction of the dog.

There was no time for its victim to react. The weight crashed into the corner, instantly snapping the pup's spine in multiple places.

Ignoring the sudden outbreak of ignorant laughter from her two older brothers, Nina stared at the twitching, twisting body of her furry friend. A thin film of water covered both eyes, and Nina's heart plummeted into her queasy belly. Soon, the last glimpse of her pet faded into a blur of gloomy colors. Shaking uncontrollably with her mouth hanging open, a hiss of air ascended from her throat. Before the scream of a real cry could emerge, Jamanny slapped her to the floor.

"You're about to cry? You're about to cry over this flea-bitten, mangy mutt!" Jamanny towered over her in dirty overalls, soaked in oil and body sweat. "Well, I'll tell you what. Since you're big and bad enough to bring a wild animal into my house, then you're big and bad enough to face the consequences of your actions. Aren't you?" He dragged her into the kitchen as the other children dashed into the adjacent room.

A long scream and the deep voice of a raving madman ricocheted through the old wooden house, reaching outside. It echoed past the rotting, roach-infested wood and corroding pipes. Miles away from any other living soul, dark secrets rattled within the bowels of the evil place, far from light or truth. When the thrashing kicks and frantic cries of a little girl rattled the window of the old grandfather clock in the living room, two mice scurried into a small opening under the kitchen sink. The warning signals ignited their keen sense of survival.

A piece of skin detached from Nina's hand and floated on top of a boiling pot of water before Jamanny released her from over the hot stove. Slipping on the wet floor, she fell backward and slid halfway under the dining room table. Scrambling to her knees, she cowered next to one of the five chairs around the dining room table. Holding her blistering hand, Nina trembled in excruciating pain. As the one who never was severely punished, she shuddered at the memories of the times she had seen her brothers and sisters get beaten to a pulp by their father.

"What is going on?" Rashida stepped into the house with groceries. "Nina? Jamanny, no!" She placed the bags on the table. "Don't, Jamanny. Let me handle it! Please?" Rashida said before being pushed to the side. "Jamanny, no. Don't!" She jumped between them a second time.

"Cook some damn food!" Jamanny shoved her to the floor in front of the kids. "Cook some damn food!"

Down, but not done, Rashida looked over at Nina's big watery eyes. Realizing that the only possible chance of saving the little girl was to take her place, she pushed herself up from the dusty floor. Shoving the old man back with all her might, she said, "I'm their mother!"

"What hell you say, woman?" Jamanny's marble eyes pumped bloodshot red as he stepped back in shock. Watching the fear and streams of tears drip from Rashida's face, he knew that she had accepted her fate. "That's what I thought you said!" He grabbed her by the neck and threw her back into the kitchen as Pig pulled Nina away. Noticing the sounds of stomping above his head, he stared at the oldest boys. They were covering their grins. "That's all right. It's okay! You can run. I got all day! All year, goddamn it! And what the hell you two goon faces laughing about?"

"What?" Timothy shrugged, leaning against the wall. "What did we do?" He looked over at his older brother, Dozer, who turned his back and looked away.

"Go feed Junior or something before I make an example outta the both of ya next!" Jamanny pointed directly at his oldest son.

Always angry, Dozer glared into his father's eyes and walked away with his brother.

Jamanny redirected his fury to Rashida. "So … you back thinking you they momma now, huh? Today, I'm a get you straight for the last and final time, woman!" He grabbed Rashida by the collar and sent her flipping over the back of the couch.

The sounds of things breaking were drowned out yelling and loud cursing. The oldest daughter, Tina, listened from the shadows of the hallway stairs. Displaced and confused, she turned her back on Rashida's suffering and proceeded to clean scattered dog feces throughout the house.

Upstairs, inside a bedroom closet, Tiger looked for a place to take a nap. Suddenly he flies out striking the bed post and runs off in a howl. Nina was in a ball along a small pallet under the cobwebbed shelves. Hanging clothes concealed her body in total darkness, hiding the hurt and throbbing pain. Sobbing over her blistering limb, Pig sat close to her, head down and arms folded.

"I told you not to bring in that dog. That's why Daddy got you!" Lamond whispered under the loud clatter that shook the walls from the first floor.

"Shut your mouth, Lamond!" snapped Pig, raising a head of thick, undone braids. "It's okay, Nina. He'll be different when he comes up here. Don't cry, okay?" Pig touched Nina's ankle as she pulled away.

"It hurts," Nina mumbled between sobs. "He killed … my … dog." Her crying intensified with Jamanny's cursing.

"He's mean. He's going to kill all of us—not just you. Stop crying." Pig peered across at her brothers who had begun to cuddle up as sounds of the downstairs battle increased. "As long as we have each other, it'll be okay, Nina." Her optimism stayed on the edge of her true feelings, but the love for her sister never wavered. Despite several occasions of hair pulling, biting, and bickering, Pig was the only one who was close to Nina.

The oldest child, Junior, was always in the basement and was forbidden to leave. Dozer and Timothy were usually kept under the helm of their father. Tina stayed in her own dark reality. Since Lamond and Omack were still too young, Pig was always by her side. "I hate him. I wish Momma was here." Nina thought of all the terrible things that Jamanny had done to them.

"Guess what? I don't like him either, but he's our father," Pig whispered.

"Aw! You called Daddy mean, and you said you hate him! I'm telling!" Lamond said. He was ready to crawl off the bed, but a loud crash changed his mind.

"If I was our mom, I would have left too." Pig touched the material of the dingy white gown that she'd worn for four days.

Nina's crying ceased with the sounds of fighting that carried deeper into the house. Perhaps taken into Jamanny's room, the fight brought a feeling of uneasiness to the children. "Why did she leave us?"

"She didn't. He killed her just like he's gonna kill us. I know because I see things that nobody else knows I see." Pig peeked into the deepness of the closet to get a better look at her sister.

Nina's head and swollen arm slowly poked out into the light.

"That's not true. You're lying." Nina held her trembling hand by her wet face.

"It is true! He murders people and keeps them in the basement. Why do you think it doesn't have a door? He feeds them to Junior, and he spits them into bones all over the basement floor. And he's not our brother; he's really a monster who eats people and little kids."

The appearance of Tina entering the doorway startled both girls.

"Hush it, you two. Right now! Pig, you can't be talking like that! He might hear you. Now close your mouths right now!" Tina said. "Nina, you're already in enough trouble. You don't want to get him any madder. What's up with you two?" She looked over at her brothers who were scared and huddling together. "It's okay, Lamond. Come here, Omack." She sat on the bed and held the boys.

"Pig says Daddy killed Momma!" Lamond blurted.

"What? Pig!" Tina hugged him tightly. "Quit making things up, Pig! Momma is alive and well!"

A door slammed and heavy footsteps approached the stairwell.

"Shhh!"

Heavy boots clunked against the steps. Pig leaped into her bed and Nina disappeared inside the closet. Tina slid to the edge of the bed, positioning Lamond and Omack behind her. The footsteps came closer, and cold chills slid down each of their bodies. Tina and Pig braced themselves.

The door to the playroom creaked open as four more steps were taken. Jamanny strode into the middle of the bedroom. The sight of him wiping blood from his hands onto a green towel sent a sickening message to the children. Wiping his dripping face with his forearm, Jamanny adjusted his trusty cap. "Tina, don't be doing no more cleaning for that gal. Ya hear me?" He scanned the room at all their faces. "Nina, get out here right now." He stared at the base of the closet, waiting for any sign of the little girl. "Come on now. Don't make me drag you out!" He jabbed an arm into the darkness between the clothes and pulled out Nina. She melted against his hand, turning her eyes to look at him bitterly. "I ain't done with your behind yet!" He sat her down. "Now when your old Poppa asks you for the truth, from now on, that's just what you give me! Do you understand me? And you are not going to keep coming to the rescue. Your day is coming." He plucked Pig on the top of the head and returned downstairs.

The front door slammed when he left the house with his two sons. They drove off in his van. Pig watched them through the cracks in the wood on one of the boarded-up windows.

A sigh broke the quietness. Tina and Pig turned their attention to the tiny sniffling murmurs of Nina. Thinking of the discomfort of her burnt hand, they both rushed to her aid.

"Come on, Nina. Let's go take care of that hand." Tina squatted and touched her hair. It was always weird for Nina to accept her help on account of her always bullying or being mean to her most of the time. When Jamanny went too far, Nina would get a glimpse of Tina's true self. She figured that there just might be the hidden potential for her to be a real big sister somewhere in there. "Come on. It's okay."

"They're gone, Nina. Tina's being nice right now!" Pig always put a sarcastic spotlight on her big sister. "Miss Rashida has medicine in her room."

"Lamond, stay up here with Omack. We'll be right back." Tina rolled her eyes at Pig and helped Nina up from the floor. "Pig, you stay here too." She thought about the bloody mess that might await them downstairs. Although they had experienced some gruesome things, there was no reason for them to continue to experience them.

"Miss Rashida's dead. He killed her," Pig whispered to Lamond with a straight face. "You heard what he said—I'm next." She slipped away behind them.

"Pig, shoot! You are hardheaded! Come on, Nina." Tina put an arm around her sister and walked to the entrance of the hall. "Be right back, you two. Be good!" She directed her little brothers from the next room as they began to play under the covers of the bed.

Closing the door behind them, Pig stood on the balls of her feet, listening with wide eyes. "I don't hear anything, Tina. There's no sound. Do you know what that means, Nina?"

"Pig, hush. Be quiet!" Tina carefully guided her down the stairs and snatched her hand away from the dried streak of blood that stretched down the remaining feet of banister.

Through the dark hall, they inched out of the shadows into the half-destroyed dining room. The table had been turned over on its side, and the chairs were scattered about in every direction. The shattered remains of plates and plastic dishes spread across the floor, leading to the kitchen. Between the narrow walkway of the kitchen, their bare feet crunched across the floor. They saw a dripping splash of blood along the edge of the counter.

Even though they were used to tragic scenes left by Jamanny, it wasn't until entering the living room that they became worried. Other than the couch being slightly shifted into the coffee table, the room appeared to be untouched. There was a long trail of blood across the floor. It looked as if someone had been dragged and pulled into Jamanny's room. How he'd always appeared calm and collected after every episode astounded them as they slowly stepped inside.

"Miss Rashida? Rashida!" Tina had a twisted, bottomless feeling on the inside of her stomach. Touching the door, she eased it open and peered into the room with watering eyes. "Rashida." The name rolled off her quivering lips.

Brutally beaten and scared, the weak and tattered body of Rashida barely moved on Jamanny's bed. She was bleeding from an open gash on her head from where Jamanny had rammed it into the edge of the kitchen counter. She was on her stomach, half-naked, spread out like an eagle. Her arms and legs were bound to the bedpost with a chain and lock. The gruesome scene stained in the children's brain. Bruises and bites complemented the rubber hose that was still wrapped around one arm, below a cluster of leaking needle holes.

Falling beside the woman, Tina burst into a frenzy of tears and cries. Looking at the only one who ever been there to care for them, Tina wiped Rashida's mouth and dabbed the blood on Rashida's head with her shirt.

The sight of the woman temporarily took away Nina's pain and refilled her with unbelievable fear. Pig walked around the uncovered mattress, holding back her tears. Even though Jamanny had tried his best to drill into their heads that Rashida wasn't their biological mother, regardless of how often he made it seem that she was the problem, Rashida was the only woman besides Tina that her siblings could remember being in their lives. The three stood over her, seeing her eyes barely opening as the homemade drugs traveled through her body, altering her perception and senses.

"Jamanny." Rashida lifted her head and dropped it against the mattress.

"Rashida, no. No, he's not here." Tina stroked her uncombed hair. "Try not to move. Your head's busted."

"Never again. It never ends. Ha!" Rashida somehow found humor in her predicament, laughing and crying at the same time. "Tina … children." She tried to reach for them, but was held back by the chains. Dozing off, she didn't move. Her face twitched as she awakened abruptly to the view of Nina. Looking down at her burnt hand, she said, "Fix her up, Tina. Get aloe out the dresser. You get to be the mama now." She grinned, and a trickle of blood dripped from her mouth.

"Don't say that, Rashida. It'll be okay—just like it always is." Tears continued to fall from Tina's face as Rashida passed out again. "Just a little bit longer, Rashida. I don't want to be the mama anymore."

Pig was inching toward the door.

"Never again shall I fear. Never shall I feel pain." Rashida closed her eyes.

"What should we do, Rashida? Where are the keys?" Tina rattled the chains and looked around the room. "Rashida, where are the keys to these locks?"

"Never again, children. Don't let him eat you. The beast is at bay, and the devil is among us. They can never get enough of hurting you. Never again. It never ends!" Rashida drifted into her other personality.

This bizarre behavior was quite normal to Nina. Out of all the years that she'd known Rashida, it was a common routine for Rashida to act out of mind after their father got a hold of her. Not knowing the drug that he was forcefully injecting into Rashida, Nina believed that he was beating her senseless. It wasn't the split personality of the woman that was bothersome; it was the question of how a person could hurt the person they love in such a manner. Nina, along with her sisters, knew that the day would come when they would share the same fate.

"It never ends!" Rashida released a loud cry that filled every room on the first floor. "The devil is among us. The devil is among us!" She swayed back and forth on the old stained mattress. "Don't let him eat you. The beast lives here too … shhhh!" She raised her index finger and blew out a gust of air. "Satan's coming … ow, my … head …"

"Rashida!" Tina noticed blood that continued to run from across Rashida's face from the gash on her head.

Pig had already gotten aid out of Rashida's dresser and was finishing a wrap on Nina's hand.

"Get me a warm wet rag and find some towels! Hurry!" She rushed to the front of the bed and pulled out a small brown case from under it. Pulling out a needle and a spool of thread, Nina finished bandaging her hand, wondering if Miss Rashida had finally reached her end.

Angry at Jamanny and helpless, Nina found strength and wiped her face, pushing back more emotions. Tina started to clear Rashida's wound. Knowing that the old man would be upset for what she'd done, she threaded the needle and held it close to Rashida's head.

"Daddy's going to be mad; he's going to kill us." Pig stood behind her, shaking her head in disbelief.

"Well, she's dying." Tina steadied her shaking hands; her entire life flashed before her. Through it all, she saw that Rashida had always been present. Pouring peroxide onto the woman's head, she shoved the needle into one side of the cut and pulled it out the opposite side of the exposed skin.

"Save her, Tina." Nina said. For the first time in a long time, they felt unified and bonded with each other. Not caring about the severity of the next punishment, they knew that they had each other. Maybe there was still a chance that they could make it out from Jamanny's rule. Against Rashida's constant bleeding, Nina and Pig stood by Tina as she attempted to repay Rashida for all the times that she wasn't able to help her.

Hours went by before the old man returned with his sons. The three girls made good use of the time by cleaning and putting things back the way they had been. Tina repaired the broken legs on one of the tables with a hammer and nails before her father could even recall ruining it. But as usual, despite their best efforts to make things right, it all went out the window when he discovered they had been in his room helping Rashida.

"Thinking you gonna run all over me! Sneaking around my house and bringing critters beyond these gates!" Furiously pointing in the direction of the front door, Jamanny, pouring sweat, unrolled a thick leather belt from his hand. After whooping Tina, Nina, and Pig, he threw his belt at her, striking her shoulder with the brass buckle. "Oh, and since we love nature so much and want to cry over them, I got a little surprise for ya!" He grabbed Nina by the hair and pulled her out of the room.

Tina was on the floor of the playroom. Jamanny looked at her in disgust as his thick forehead muscles cast a deep shadow over his pupils. Stomping his boot, Tina's black and blue body jumped and smacked nervously against the floor. Moving her sore neck to raise her head, she glanced up as the door slammed shut behind them. Practically dragging Nina down the halls to the front door, Jamanny stormed out of the house with her in his grip.

From the side of the house, Nina could see Dozer and Timothy following a few feet behind.

"Okay Nina, pussycat, you want to make new friends? Well, Daddy's brought home a friend for you to meet! You're going to make such great pals." He dragged her to the backyard.

Trying her best to keep up with the pace of Jamanny's long legs, Nina stumbled over rocks and potholes in the soil. Between every second and third step, she lost her footing, but managed to regain her balance. While keeping a tight fixture on Jamanny's hand, Nina tried to avoid getting clumps of hair pulled out like during previous times. Despite a few loose farm animals running wild, outside the house was like a jungle, untamed and uncut.

The few times that Nina had been allowed out, she had never seen half of the things that she heard moving around her. Thrown forward, she fell into thickets of bushes and thorny weeds.

"Meet your new best friend—Mr. Tiny." Jamanny walked away laughing.

Dozer watched with a troubled face. Timothy tried to contain his giggling anticipation of a next good laugh or call to action.

Opening her eyes, Nina lifted up from the dirt and looked back at her so-called relatives. Returning forward, she looked around puzzled, only seeing grass. Thinking maybe she was just the butt of another one of her father's cruel jokes, Nina stood as her entire body centered on an extremely large dog—a pit bull mastiff.

Sinking into the beast's black eyes, Nina felt her soul flee into the house and hide with her sisters. Almost triple her size, the canine shook his head and sniffed loudly in disapproval. Dingy with whitish fur, the large mongrel snarled an enormous set of teeth at her. Letting loose the scream of a person getting murdered as the dog leaped back, Nina darted off in the opposite direction. Passing her father and Timothy, the barking rumbled through her bones and weakened her legs as she fell down on the grass.

"He's tied to a post, dummy! He just wants to play," Jamanny said, observing the tied end of the dog's restraint. He snatched the wooden post into the air, free of the ground.

Flipping over, Nina watched Mr. Tiny come at her in slow motion. With skin flapping around its mighty jaws, she braced for her face to be ripped apart by his teeth. Then, as if gravity had reversed its polarity, the animal reverted back as Dozer wrestled hold of the chain and snatched the large dog.

"What the? And where do you think you're going?" Jamanny's face turned red as Nina ran to the house. "Dozer, did I tell you to get that dog, boy? Huh?" He took off his cap and swatted Dozer across the head as he held the barking dog. "Shut the hell up!" He kicked the dog as the animal bit him on the leg, breaking free of his son's grip. "Goddamn it, Doza!"

Timothy rambled to himself, quite frightened by the loose hound.

Hearing them calling the wild animal in the distance, Nina could hear the rattling of the dog's chain and the rustling of his paws approaching behind her. Hollering for her sisters to open the front door, Nina cut around the side of the building. Imagining the hundreds of pounds of muscle and teeth on her heels, she made it to the front door as it cracked open. Shutting the door at the sight of the dog approaching like a freight train, Nina braced against the old wooden latch with her sisters.

As the dog slammed into the cracking wood, the door started to come off its hinges. Jerking and bobbing forward, keeping the dog from entering the house, the three realized that things had gotten a bit worse as Nina wished they were with their mother.

Chapter 5:
THE STATE OF JAMANNY

———————— ❉ ————————

The sun beamed down on the air that sat still on the shoulders of anything that wasn't under the shade or the coolness of an air conditioner. The smell of dead things mixed with the twang of flowers and green plants that seemed to retake the acres and acres of Jamanny's land. An old rooster crowed from behind a hidden shabby house. Barn animals that had lived happily among the farms roamed free among the trees behind the old fences and fields. A variety of fish swam up and down creeks, searching for food and algae.

Inside his rusty blue van, Jamanny marveled at his unkempt property, rekindling the day when the world seemed to have taken everything for him. Not caring about life or nature, he smiled at the blood taste of satisfying revenge that had once waged against the person that he loved and hated so much. Having lost her to his ignorant ways and intolerable habits that he refused to let go of, he secretly tormented three generations of a woman's family until death became his preferred tool. With his fury quenched, Jamanny rode off happily into the rest of his life with his two sons.

Dozer rode shotgun while Timothy sat behind his father.

"It's a wonderful world, boys!" Jamanny patted Dozer on the shoulder twice. "This will all be yours one day, fellas. Miles and miles of uncharted land, built by hard work and muscle. Now what's wrong with your face, Doza? It's a good day today!" He took his eyes completely off the road to look at his son. "Are you disappointed or mad about something, boy?"

"He don't want to roll with us no more, Pops." Timothy playfully patted the top of Dozer's head and threw a punch at him.

"Man, shut up, Timothy! Nobody's even talking to you!" Dozer snapped. "You always want to answer for somebody! You always—"

"Doza! Timothy, close your mouth, son!" Jamanny said. "So what's the problem, Doza? And Timothy, don't you say a dang word!"

"I just want more, Daddy. I mean, what is this? Ain't the world bigger than this?" Dozer gazed into the passing woods and then down at his rough hands, which looked exactly like his father's.

"I just want more?" Jamanny hissed and smirked. "Boy, let me tell you something. It don't get no better than this. When you get out there, you're gonna be forced to live by lies and rules that even the ones who make them break. I don't know about you, boy, but to me, that ain't no kind of world that I want to be a part of." Jamanny took one hand off the steering wheel and slung his cap into a collection of dirty caps on the dash. "This land right here—I worked for it, from your age and younger. Hand over hand, foot over foot. Me and my family slowly acquired it—piece by piece, plot by plot—until it was ours. One day, the white man came in his fancy suits and took it away with their fancy papers and technical babble! We didn't have nothing. I took it back—every part of it! I'm trying to learn ya something, boy. This means something. You already got what they trying to get! We make the rules, and you can tell anybody to get the fuck off the property!" He laughed a barrage of coughs and smacked the wheel.

"Dad, that's your dream—not mine. What if I want to be a doctor or a mechanic?"

"Did he say that's my dream?" Jamanny asked Timothy, looking directly through the rearview mirror. Confirming the words, his blood pressure began to rise. "Now Doza, you really pushin' it! Just a little too beside yourself now! We having a good day. I think I'm—"

A man walking away from a house caught his attention.

"I don't believe this! Who the hell is this? Boys, it's time for a new lesson." He drove near the man and parked the van. "Get out!" He pointed at both doors and climbed between the front seats to the back.

"Dad? This is stupid." Dozer scratched his head and slammed the door.

"All right!" Timothy jumped out the vehicle and whispered, "What's the plan? What are we doing, Pops?" He watched another person appear in back of the man and approached his brother. Looking for his father to appear from behind the van, Timothy turned, chuckled, and said, "Can we help you?" He put on his best serious act, moving in front of the vehicle.

Dozer remained quiet.

The professionally dressed man carrying a small black briefcase stepped forward. An African American woman swayed behind him.

"Hello. Are you guys from around here? We're just looking for any sign of life. According to our records, there are numerous families and children that live in this area. Can you tell us why it's always so vacant? We must've driven around here dozens of times; every house is boarded up or empty." The man held his hand out for a handshake, but the brothers looked at it like a foreign object. "I'm sorry. We're social workers. We're just going down our list, looking for families and children who might be in need of services. You know that life can be harsh sometimes."

"So-shall workers huh? Hey, Pops, they says they're so-shall workers." Timothy sniggled at his pronunciation.

"Stand aside and let grown people talk, boys." Jamanny emerged from behind the van.

"How can I help you? Or better yet, why don't you just repeat those finely spoken words?"

"Hi, we're from Social Services, and we're looking for a slew of families that live here but, apparently don't, or haven't been here for a real long time. Can you help us out? Where is everyone?"

The woman stepped between them to ease the approach.

"Bonjour and howdy to you too. Aren't we a beauty?" Jamanny looked the woman up and down. "Sorry, but this here town's been deserted for years—had some kinda toxic scare. Maybe you should try the next town. It's about four hundred miles back yonder. The city of Sardis is full of people, altogether too. Try your luck there."

"Toxic scare?" The man wiped his sweating head. Beginning to feel ill, he touched his queasy stomach and stepped a few paces back. "Maybe you can help cross a few families off the list?"

"Do you know or have you heard of the Johnsons, the Fowler family, or the Durgens?" the woman asked, reading from a clipboard.

Glancing over at his sons, Jamanny said, "No, we don't know any off those folks. Why don't you try your luck down the road?" He slowly walked to the back of the van, leaving the two social workers.

The woman showed her partner some black and white photos in the profiles, and he identified Jamanny as the head of the Durgen family. "Jamanny Durgen—wait. We need to talk!" The man eyed the two filthy boys and stepped past them. "We'd like to assist your family. Isn't this your picture? Mr. Jamanny Durgen?"

"Yep," Jamanny said as the man's head exploded in all directions from an unforeseen blast from the old man's rifle.

As the woman screamed in terror, Dozer pulled a glob of the man's brain from out of his right eye socket and stormed off to the van. "Bullshit!"

Covered in blood and tissue, Timothy laughed hilariously at his brother and the screaming woman. He was proud to be with his father.

Reloading his hunting rifle, Jamanny raised it a second time and pointed it directly at the screaming woman. "Enough about me—let's talk about you."

"Please, don't kill me! I have kids and a family! I'm just doing my job!" Mascara dripped down the woman's face as she trembled and shielded herself with the notebook. "Please, I'll do anything you want! Please!" She prayed that he could be reasoned with.

"You know, as pretty and as fine as you are, I think that you are one of the worst types of people on the face of this miserable planet. You stand here in fear of losing your life, crying about your kids, when you plainly come to take mine away from me! Shut that goddamn crying up!"

He opened the gun's breech and tossed the spent cartridge onto the ground, replacing it with a new round. He closed the bolt and walked up to the woman, returning to the front of the van. "You wasn't doing all of that crying all of those months that you and your boyfriend here was looking for me and my family. Well, I'm here, and I'm mighty glad you found me. Social Services on my property, on my land, miles away from home! See, sons, this is a prime example of how city slickers come to split up the family of the common man. Nobody—and I do mean nobody—will ever come between me and my castle." He pointed the gun at her mouth as Dozer moved the rifle away.

"Daddy, don't kill her!" Dozer looked into the innocent woman's eyes with remorse.

"Kill her? Now why the hell would I want to do that?" Jamanny lowered the gun, scratched his chin, and stared past a house into a nearby field.

Somewhere else upon the property, behind a group of abandoned houses, just beyond the creek and inside an unusual patch of woods, the three Durgens spent their next hours. Carrying two shovels from the van, Dozer, marched behind his father, dragging the dead body.

Dozer hadn't spoken a word since he saved the woman. "Dad, this is what I'm talking about. This is wrong right here! Again! We're going to go to jail or worse. Dad, we're going to burn in hell!" Dozer dropped the body onto the soft grass. "See, I been readin' the Bible, and it says we're breaking one of the rules in it. One of GOD's rules." He rested his hands on his waist and caught his breath. "Daddy, you can't keep killin' people. We're gonna get stopped sooner or later!"

"Come on, son. Tear it up, and let's get going!" Jamanny yelled over at Timothy, who had the other social worker, bent over against a tree, pinned with her suit dress stretching completely over her head. "Who are we supposed to be getting busted by, Doza? Who? Tell me, I'll even let you whisper it into my ear." Slightly agitated, Jamanny peered at his tired son, "Who's gonna come looking? The police?" He picked up a shovel and pointed it to a dull patch of dirt. "Or you think some type of fire department is coming?" His long thick fingers aimed at an area where the grass grew in a patchy, distinct row. "Here, we got city workers, state workers, clerks, bankers, inspectors, mailmen, Boy Scouts, Girl Scouts, and Cub Scouts! Hell, this one even owed me ten dollars." Jamanny spit at the ground after completing a full spin of pointing. And it wasn't until he showed his son the last plot that it all registered. To Dozer, this was years of senseless murder. "So they all can come. Bring them all! I'll send them straight to hell first!" He waved his rifle in the air and dropped the shovel.

"But it's wrong, Daddy! Look at us, we're covered in blood. This is bananas! I thought we only did this together? When did you do all of this? How? And why?" He looked around. "I should work—and have a job just like you once did! Not this! Maybe I want to get married, earn, and build off my own land just like you, Daddy." He stood up and looked his father in the eyes.

"Time's up, boy. Bring her on! I don't got all day!" Turning his back on Dozer, Jamanny flagged Timothy.

"I'm coming. I'm coming! I creamed her real good too, Pops—just like you showed me. Look, she can barely stand!" Timothy zipped up his jeans and pulled the crying woman from behind the tree.

"Son, I think you done did it a little too good. She's still dripping!" Jamanny nudged Timothy on the shoulder and pushed the woman down to the ground. "Move those bushes, Doza!" He pointed at a stack of dead branches and leafy stems. "Just shove them off to the side."

Removing the large clump of thickets, Dozer uncovered a large hole, five feet long and three feet wide. "This isn't? Dad?" He then noticed an anthill looking mound of dirt next to a nearby tree. "Dad, you said you wouldn't kill her!"

"Boy, what's wrong with you? I'm not going to kill her." Jamanny tossed the gun to Timothy.

"Timothy, don't shoot that dang gun! Dad, we can't do this anymore! You're going to get in trouble, and they're going to take you away! We could get split up! They got all kinds of high technology now. There are all kinds of ways to catch criminals. We could be doing something else with our lives—something productive!" Stuck on how his life could be different and meaningful, Dozer attempted to talk reason into his bullheaded father.

"Let me go, please. I did what you asked! Please!" The woman made her way to Jamanny's leg. "I'm just a caseworker! We were trying to give your family free services! Please don't do this." She turned and cried hysterically at the empty plot beside her.

"You know what?" Jamanny snatched his leg away from the woman. "To me, it's beginning to sound like you gettin' pretty smart, don't ya think, boy?" He walked over to Timothy and snatched the rifle. "It sounds like you've been reading? You been reading, Doza? Been going to school lately, boy?" The rifle scope rose to Dozer's eye level. Growing weary of his son, Jamanny finger trembled on the trigger and pills poured into his dry, wrinkled mouth.

"What? No, Dad. I ain't been to no school, and I ain't been reading! I promise you, Daddy!" Dozer feared the mad stare of his father. Feeling the cold seriousness of the face, he slightly changed his tune. "Nah, Dad, I swear."

"Yep, yo ass been readin' something besides the Bible," Jamanny said while locking in dirty looks. The woman made a desperate attempt to run for safety as her right calf was blown right from under her. Jamanny's nostrils flared and his eyes flushed with red. "Let me tell you something, boy." He walked over to the crawling woman and pushed her small body into the ground. "You best be watching what's coming out your mouth! Cause if I find out somebody's been learnin' ya, I'll drop you where you stand, boy." He threw the rifle at Dozer. "I done told you that I don't want you picking up nothing that this world has to offer. It's bullshit—lies—and my kids are only going to learn what I teach them, me, Jamanny C. Durgen!"

He slapped his chest and heard the woman screaming for help. Leaning over the hole at the puffy eyes of the woman, he smiled at Dozer. "Now finish the job, son." Jamanny found the shovel to hit his son with if he didn't comply.

And in an instance, all of Dozer's hopes and goals of a better life flushed down the drain, replaced by bad memories of evil deeds that his father had made him do. Picturing his father crawling in the woman's place, half slaughtered and dying, the woman reached for him as he fired into the open earth. Tears fled from their ducts, leaving Dozer in the silence of the woods.

"You ever hesitate again, boy, I'll kill you," Jamanny whispered behind his ear. "Now let's get them covered before supper." He took the gun and gave Dozer the shovel. As Timothy picked up the other, he directed him to drag the man's body closer to another covered grave.

Walking back to the hole that the woman was in, Jamanny looked down at her splattered body and lit a cigarette. "Damn, you didn't get you none of that. She was cute!"

Jamanny watched Dozer dig the shovel into the dirt and shook his head. As he watched his son, Dozer pretended he was burying the crazed old man.

And while Dozer and Timothy fulfilled their father's awful deeds, the daughters tended to his daily requirement of keeping the house in order. Rashida's job was to do the overall cleaning and to prepare dinner while Tina gave her a hand and washed the walls. Pig had to sweep and mop the upstairs, and Nina had the same task downstairs. The house was filled with the clanging of dishes, splashing of water, and the continuous scrubbing of firm bristles against hard wood. Along with the occasional griping and secret complaining, the small distinct pitter-patter of Omack and Lamond dashing in and out of rooms broke the tension of hard work.

"The water is more red than usual today." Nina, on her hands and knees, dipped a small scrubbing brush into a bucket.

Tina envisioned the beatings that took place in that same exact spot, blocking them out her mind. "Just do it, Nina." Against the wall on a small wooden stool that wobbled on its uneven leg, she wiped down the walls with a wet cloth. When her legs began to buckle and her good arm began to tremble, she covered her nose and mouth from the fumes of her father's homemade cleaning agents.

Putting all her energy into the down motion of the scrub, Nina concentrated on covering the most area possible. From the hall that led upstairs, up to the walkway of the kitchen, the floorboards slowly began to look like a real wood floor again. Falling on top of the dampness, Nina rolled over, out of breath and spunk. Letting loose of the brush, she held up her tired arms and made a face at the sight of the splinters that were embedded in her hands and forearm. "I hate this place."

A sudden movement in the corner of her eye caught her attention. Slowly turning her head to the view of Rashida having a full conversation with herself, Nina awaited the full transformation of Rashida into that other person. It was almost every day that Nina witnessed this happen. Although Nina had little understanding of why Rashida floated in out of the realm of insanity, the woman was still quite a spectacle to see. "Miss Rashida's acting crazy," she whispered in the direction of her sister.

"You know what? I'm finished. I'm not doing anymore. I'm tired." Tina stepped down into a bucket of dirty water. "Great."

"I'm done." Pig entered the room soaking wet, half drenched in bubbles.

"How are you done that fast? You're really done with every single thing, Pig?" Tina sat on the stool and rested against the wall. "You know Daddy's gonna beat the mess outta you if you're not finished."

"I think I'd rather take a beating. We're going to get a whooping anyway." Pig wrung out her gown onto the wet floor. "And what about you? How come there's dirt still on the walls?" Her sweaty, undone braids hung around her face. Looking up at her big sister's serious face, Tina surprised her with a faint smile, which made them both laugh.

"Tina? Pig? Tina!" Nina softly called as she watched Rashida double over and dash off like an animal into the back rooms, leaving a pot of spaghetti boiling over. "Hey!" Nina slid the scrub brush across the floor in her sister's direction. Bumping the edge of Pig's bare foot, the brush simmered down the conversation and caused Pig to look in Nina's direction. Signaling them, she stood up, darting off into the kitchen as they slowly followed. "Tina!" Nina called, frantically searching for the correct burner on the stovetop to turn off. As the hot pot bubbled and boiled, it pooled and overflowed onto the floor.

"Uh-oh." Pig spotted a light cloud of smoke floating out of the kitchen and saw Tina flying by her.

"Oh my goodness, Rashida!" Tina turned the burner down and regained control of the situation. "Where is she? Where'd she go that fast?" Tina grabbed some kitchen towels and wiped the stove and floor.

"I dunno? She's super crazy today! First, she was just standing there talking, and then she squatted and ran off like an animal!" Nina peeked into the living room, making sure that Rashida couldn't hear her. "She just went down on her hands and feet—and ran off just like that. She's crazy."

"She got into Daddy's drugs again," Pig said from behind them.

"Pig! Shut up! Just leave it alone!" Tina tried to change the subject.

"You can't hide it from us forever, Tina. It's in front of us every day. Sometimes Daddy makes her use drugs and, other times, when she's feeling bad, she takes them herself." Pig said as Tina attempted to cover her mouth.

"Take what, Pig? You don't really even know what you're talking about!" Tina returned to stirring the pot. "She's not on drugs all the time."

"Most of the time." Pig walked into the living room. "So where'd she go?"

"What are drugs?" Nina asked as Tina shook her head.

"There are things we take to feel good, but they are really, really bad for us. If you ever come across them, don't ever try them! They're against the law." Tina turned off the stove. "We're gonna have to make another pot. This is gummed up and burnt." She closed the lid with a loud clang and moved to the living room.

"How do you two know about drugs? Wait, who told you?" Nina asked Tina gave her the evil eye.

"Look, one day, I'll show you. Let's just forget about it for right now, okay?" Tina peered at Nina. Her mind was blown by how smart her little sisters were for their ages.

"It's quiet. I don't hear anything, and she's not in Dozer's room. Think she's in your Daddy's room?" Pig stood in the hallway.

"He's your dad too," Tina said to Pig. "And no, we're not going in there."

"I don't want to go back in there, Pig!" Nina pictured her father's mad face and thought about the floor that she hadn't finished scrubbing. "I'm going back. We're going to get in trouble." The sound of something breaking made them all jump back. "She's in here."

"Rashida." Feeling somewhat responsible for the woman every time she acted unlike herself, Tina's guilt crept down over her shoulders, waiting for the next time when she had to stand by and watch Jamanny put his hands on Rashida.

"What if the monster got her and took her body into the basement?" Pig's eyes widened with fear and curiosity as she glanced down the hall at her father's door.

"Pig!" snapped Tina.

"The basement? You mean downstairs—under the house? Nobody knows where the door is, remember? We've been looking for it for years." Nina twisted her lips and moved closer to her sisters.

"No one knows where the door is but, Daddy, Dozer, Timothy, and Miss Rashida. If the monster didn't get her, maybe we can get her to show us the door so we can find Mommy? Her body's got to be down there." With nerves of steel, Pig exhaled and prepared for the worst.

"Will you shut up already? Our mother's not dead under the house! And Miss Rashida wasn't taken by some boogeyman!" Tina's finger touched Pig's nose. "You don't know what happened to Momma, and you don't even know for sure if there is really a downstairs! Now, we need to get Rashida, finish our chores, and try not to get our butts kicked! So if you don't mind, Pig, stop telling her that stuff before she starts believing it!" Tina smacked her mouth and walked toward Jamanny's room.

"I believe it," Pig said.

Having a bad feeling about being in that hall, Nina folded her arms as Pig took one of her hands and pulled her. The hall was always dark and grim. She always thought of the blood that had been spilled there. Usually captivated by its mystery, Nina had loved playing in there, and it was just as scary to her then as it was now. Dozer's room met them at the entrance, followed by Timothy's room, and then their father's room at the far end of the hall. Stretching out her hand, Nina touched a shelf of miscellaneous silhouettes of things that accompanied a set of empty shelves along the wall. Remembering how stained that area was, she pulled away her hand and wiped it on her dress.

Tina opened their father's door as Tiger leaped out at her leg. Screaming, she calmed herself at the sight of the cat running up the hall. Calming, she looked into the room. Stepping back and closing the door, Tina sent a slamming sound bouncing down the hall. "Okay, she's not in there."

"Wow." Pig received a chill along with the thought of a monster living in the house.

In front of Timothy's room, Nina's arm reached out, hand open, and spread it around the doorknob. Before turning, she hoped that when they found Miss Rashida, she would be the friendly version instead of the violent and wild one. Nina knew that—even if her better personality was present—taking caution was always advised.

Cracking the door, Nina released the knob as it loosely opened into the darkness, disappearing in a quiet, settling swing. Tina's face had begun to look a little worried. Nina slid one arm outside the doorframe and turned on the light. A circular, spinning spark of light inside the old bulb popped with the illumination of hundreds of fluffy white feathers floating freely around Timothy's room. Covering the messy sheets and torn covers that hung off the bed, the piles of light feathers moved and swayed across the floor and over his dresser and chair. What appeared almost heavenly suddenly became a scene of eeriness.

"Look." Nina pointed to an old lamp that was shattered to pieces next to the bed. "Did Miss Rashida do this?"

"All I know is I didn't do it, but we're all going to get blamed." Tina moved her out the way.

"Yeah. Daddy's going to kill us." Pig looked around and sighed. Moving to the left of the bed, she stared at the mess. "We're going to clean all of this?"

"But we found it this way?" Feathers collected on top of Nina's head. The thud of a small rubber ball bouncing in the hall across from the room caught her attention. "Did you see that?" She wiped her itchy eyes at the sight of the ball rolling past the doorway.

"See what? What was it?" Tina held up two of her brother's empty pillow cases from the piles of feathers on the bed.

"It was a ball; it just rolled from somewhere." Nina sneezed three times before a low horrible moan snuck into their ears and imagination. "Did y'all hear that?" She moved back from the door, closer to the bed.

"Okay, that was loud!" Tina froze in place over the bed.

"Junior must've gotten out and eaten Rashida. He's down here! The monster! We're next." Pig balled up her fist as Nina released an awesome screech.

Nina suddenly fell to the floor as Tina screamed and ran to her aid. "Help me. Grab me!" A pair of cold hands seized Nina by the ankles. Screaming for her life, a great force began to pull Nina under the bed. It scratched her skin, shook the bed, and filled the room with growls and snarls. Thinking of nothing but her mother, tears shot out from the corners of Nina's eyes. Watching her sister desperately pull on both arms, Nina slowly slipped away, disappearing behind a cloud of feathers inside the darkness under the bed. "Let me go. Let me go!"

Nina burst into an uncontrollable laughter, receiving a tickling sensation around her ribs and under her arms. Kicking and barely escaping, Nina slid out as her sisters looked at each other dumbfounded. After Nina pulled herself up, Rashida popped from under the bed, lifting the box-spring and mattress from the frame on her back.

Tina and Pig jumped back as Rashida stepped from under the bed and flying feathers smiling, with her pupils dilated beyond their normal size. "Fooled you!" She laughed hysterically, dropping the bed in place behind her. "Ah, the children, so precious. Tina, Nina, and little Piglet." She hugged Tina, nearly toppling over in the process.

"Hold on, Rashida. Be careful." Tina braced her by the waist. "I got you. Look at this mess, Rashida. Did you do this? Daddy's going to get us again." She helped Rashida to the doorway.

Leaning, Rashida slid down the wall into a squatting position. Lowering her head between her knees, she plopped down onto her rump. Tilting back, she closed her eyes, smiled, and let loose a short spurt of giggles and tears. "I'm gonna get my laugh. I'm gonna get my laugh!"

"Rashida, we don't have time for this! Daddy is probably on his way back. He's going to hurt us badly if we don't quit playing around!" Tina, relieved that they had found her, grew concerned about her current fate.

A little worried, Nina looked down at the large luggage that Rashida carried under her eyes, following the dents to the scars that zigzagged and crisscrossed her face. Usually when Rashida had reached her peak with the house and Jamanny, the best way to calm her down was to talk. "What's wrong, Miss Rashida?" Nina said in a calm voice and touched her.

Laughing for two seconds, Rashida looked at Nina with rolling tears. "Precious little Nina." She took Nina's wrinkled hand and looked at Pig blankly. "Tired, so tired. But never again, I'm gonna get my laugh."

Stooping beside Nina, Tina gently took Rashida's chin and directed it toward her. Looking into her eyes, she sensed how bad the drugs were taking over. "We have to go, Rashida. Daddy's coming." She reached for her arm as Rashida moved away.

"My babies ... never again." Rashida looked at Tina's deformed arm and cried even harder, visualizing being beaten next to Tina when Jamanny allowed his deceased son Jamondo to break it. Picturing all the times that she had been present yet useless during the children's time of need, she remembered being bloody on a table as Jamanny aborted her unborn child over and over again. "Never again shall I fear. Never again shall I feel pain. Never again! Gotta run or fight until the death of your soul." She bumped the back of her head against the wall twice.

"What? Come on. What are you talking about, Rashida?" Tina made little sense of the words as Nina listened quietly. Pig drew closer.

"She slayed the demon. Her eyes were so evil but holy. She was so beautiful. I loved him. He was mine. How dare she?" Rashida snickered and frowned at Nina. "The demon poisons our mind and she was so pretty ... freed us. Now all that remains ... all that lives ... is the devil and the monster." She paused at a deep dark, faraway howl that penetrated the floor, followed by a pounding sound from somewhere in the house.

They all froze in place, staring out the door, at the opposite wall across the hall. Nina's eyes widened to their fullest capacity as she suddenly felt a vibration from under her feet, deep below the house.

"The monster!" Pig slid behind Tina. "He's gonna eat us."

"Pig!" Tina nudged her arm and whispered, "You're not helping!"

"Junior!" Nina said. In a cold sweat, she rekindled once when Junior got loose. Usually locked away and forbidden to be seen for some reason, on this particular day, with brute force, he made it from the basement to the hall that led upstairs. Coming into view, Nina had watched him make it to the steps, growling and screaming as Timothy ordered her and their siblings to go back into the room. As Dozer and their father wrestled Junior back down, Nina remembered catching the first and last glimpse of the back of his large head.

"Miss Rashida!" Tina's call interrupted Nina's nightmarish flashback, bringing her back to their drug abusive caretaker.

What Rashida was trying to tell them, and Pig's uncertain knowledge of her mother's whereabouts under the house, drowned in Nina's fears while eating at her curiosity. Only one question stood out in her mind. "Where is the door to downstairs?" She gazed at the woman's bobbling head and barely opened eyes. Nervously, Nina and her sisters watched

Rashida's movements. Along with a split personality, when on drugs, she was also known for lashing out or becoming irrational when asked too many random questions.

"No, Nina. Stop it!" Tina shook her head in disagreement. "I don't want you going down there."

"Miss Rashida! Can you hear us? We need to know where the basement is. How do you get down there?" Pig blurted, dodging Tina's swings. Curious to see death and to know the truth about their mother drove her to speak—and Nina to join in—despite the consequences.

"We need your help, Miss Rashida. Where is the door to the basement?" Nina got in her face. As Tina pushed her back, Rashida opened her eyes.

"The door, the ... to the ... no, child! Cold, alone, you don't want to go down there." Rashida nodded off again as she whispered, "The devil's kitchen."

"See! Let's just get her up and go! We gotta clean up before Daddy comes!" Tina got ready to move the woman; Nina jumped over her with watery eyes.

"Rashida, no! This is our only chance! We don't gotta be alone. You could go with us!" Nina was determined to find the remains or a trace of her mother. She resisted the grip of her older sister.

"Tina, wait!" Pig rushed Tina to the floor before she had a chance to punch her. "Miss Rashida, you can take us to the devil's kitchen and help us find a way to beat Satan!" Pig nudged Rashida's arm as her head fell to her shoulder and her body collapsed.

In front of the three puzzled sisters, Rashida's body began to shake and jolt sporadically. Her mouth foamed white bubbles, leaking yellow fluids. Her legs banged against the floor, sending the young girls into a panic over the episode.

"What is she doing? What do we do? Rashida!" Nina yelled.

"I don't know! Rashida!" All types of thoughts and emotions toward the woman went through the teenager's mind. "No!" Tina blocked Rashida's head from hitting the floor.

Pig stood over them, watching every second of the coming of what she thought was death. Embracing it in a way, a sudden feeling of a remorseful cold overcame her as Rashida's breathing slowed and stopped. Pig peered over the woman with her sisters. "She's dead; isn't she?" Pig wiped her face and turned away.

"Hear that?" Rashida jumped up, sending the three screaming backward. "My babies!" Rashida leaped to her feet and ran off into the hall. Three slams of various doors made them flinch.

"She ran off? Go … get … her." Tina, holding her beating heart, pushed Nina to the side and gave Pig one of her famous evil looks. "We had her right here!"

"Where'd she go this time?"

Pig was creeping into the hall.

"I think she went into Daddy's room." Pig gazed down the hall at his door. "Rashida!" she called, receiving no response.

"Come on!" Tina grumbled off behind Rashida as her sisters followed. "I heard three doors close, Rashida! There's only two doors in Daddy's room—this one and the closet!" She burst into the room.

"The closet—she has to be in the closet." Pig skimmed the cluttered, unholy room of her father. With clothes and newspapers thrown all over the place, a bed with chains and rope draped around the legs sat uncovered in the middle of the room. The only other furniture to occupy the room was a tall dresser to the right of the bed, just feet away from the closet. "Uh-oh, she's going to try to scare us again." Pig peeped under the bed and moved in front of the closet door.

"We don't have time for this! Rashida, come out here now!" Tina swung open the closet door as a cool breeze of mildew and stench blew across their face and noses. "Rashida? Rashida?" She slid clothes, boxes, and shoes around. "She's not in here."

"I never knew Daddy's closet was so big. Where'd she go?" Pig shoved her way past Tina's hips, wiggling into the dark closet.

"Maybe she didn't come in here. Maybe it just sounded like she did. What if she's trying to trick us?" Nina stood before the crooked entrance, behind her sisters.

"She's not trying to trick us." Tina folded her arms.

"What's in here?" Nina squatted at the base of the closet. "It's dark in there. I can't even see you, Pig. Where you at? Pig?" She stared into the blackness, under the old jackets, just above stacks of black garbage bags of clothes and paper.

"Pig!" Tina stepped into the closet, stuck out one hand, and began to separate the clothes. Being still for a moment, she heard a distant buzzing and sudden movement. "Pig?"

"Get in here. I found it!" Pig's muffled voice echoed inside the darkness of the closet. The sisters glanced at each other with surprise and dove toward her voice.

Unable to see anything, Tina and Nina felt their way around the dark cramped space with their hands and feet. As Nina stretched her arm out, rubbing the back wall with her hand, it vanished, and a cold draft took its place.

"Pig?" Nina whispered. She shrieked in fright as a pair of small cold hands yanked her arm into the emptiness. Automatically pulling Tina with her, they stumbled over a cluster of Jamanny's work boots. Another lonely bulb flickering for life above hanging bands of wires and cords met them on the other side of the narrow hall.

"She's down there. I heard her." Pig stood in the hall at the edge of the wooden floorboards that led to another case of wooden stairs.

"The basement." Nina touched a large flapping board that was hinged up to the outside of Jamanny's closet. She could see how it could have been easily mistaken for a wall.

"I don't believe this." Tina stood up and walked next to Pig. "You two stay here. Guess I'm going to get her." She took a deep breath and went down the stairs.

"Right." Pig gave her a sarcastic look and stepped down the stairs immediately after her.

Nina carefully followed them as her heart beat nervously. A buzzing sound of popping electricity ran into bulbs that began to await them every ten to fifteen feet. The stairwell descended in a spiral motion into the earth. Nina watched the floor and base of the house disappear into dirt and stone. Deep under the house, the path grew damp and cold as the lighting dimmed. The wall around them went from wood to earth. It was composed of black mold and filthy brick that housed a variety of critters and insects.

The wood stairs and railing connected to a staircase of drywall, brick, and iron toward the end of the last flight of stairs. Water dripped against knocking pipes from inside the walls, past wires that were temporarily affixed to the ceiling and walls with staples and old nails.

Holes of all sizes decorated the patterns of black bricks that Nina managed to make out with her eyes. Old dry blood soaked into the dirt and floor, forming black skids and splashes in every which way. Dead bugs hugged in ancient webs as the carcasses of flies and wiggling maggots crunched and popped under their feet.

"Rashi—" Nina started to scream as Pig covered her mouth with both hands.

"Don't yell!" Pig uncovered Nina's mouth. "The monster will hear us. Remember?" She stopped in a walkway, facing a metal door that had been welded shut. "He lives down here."

"That monster that you're talking about is our brother, you know? Stop calling him a monster. He has a name! Junior!" Tina said. Turning left, she faced a long corridor of doors. Boards of lumber were the walls or helped patch them along with aluminum sheets. Tina sighed in disappointment. "Pig, I think you're right. Daddy's going to kill us." She peered at her sisters and inched down the dark hall.

"Where could she have run off so fast?" Nina felt uncertain about proceeding until Pig took her hand.

"I guess we should start in these stupid rooms." Tina began to try different doors as her sisters joined her.

Some doors remained closed; others, each more horrifying than the next, easily opened with a twist of the wrist. The rooms were filthy and unsanitary; traces of past tortures haunted every inch of space. With the flip of a switch or a pull of a string, the rooms instantly illuminated with horror scenes of animals, flesh, bones, and displays of remains that maintained their own level of sick mystery. Tiny squeaks of rodents dissipated as a door creaked open to the view of some type of large carcass, savagely mutilated and scattered all over an old office table and floor.

Tina covered her mouth as the stench instantly turned her stomach. At the sight of all the gore, Pig maintained the permanent grin of a mental patient. Nina watched her closely, pushing on another door, connecting to some unknown brutal past.

A pair of familiar eyes met Nina's under the dim ceiling light. Hairless, scuffed, and covered in mud, the face of a doll primarily remained intact. Inside a room of stacked broken tables and chairs of all sizes, she walked up to a large table in the center.

"The bulb's blown." Pig tried turning a switch on a lamp behind her. Unscrewing the bulb, she held it up to her ear and shook it.

With the hallway as their only source of light, Nina placed her hands upon the rim of the table and skimmed the area for the rest of the doll's body. Vaguely remembering receiving the doll at another time, in another place, she felt something cold, wet, and sticky upon her fingertips. Examining the dark liquid, she accidentally bumped a leg out from under the table, sending it crashing to the floor, just missing both of her feet. Busted and poorly sewn together, the doll's head rolled inches before the door, leaking a dark trail of red. Quickly moving back in disgust, Nina noticed large bite marks embedded around its face. She exited with her sister, slamming the door.

"I bet these are the monster's playrooms," Pig said in a low tone.

Nina just peered at her in confusion.

"This is silly, Rashida!" Tired of Rashida's immature spells, Tina began yelling for her. "Rashida, come on!" Her voice echoed down the hall.

"Hope you know we're going to get eaten. You're too loud," Pig whispered.

Hearing laughter and a loud bang, Tina ran off. "I'm going to get Rashida; you two go back upstairs!" The heel of Tina's right foot vanished behind her. Her bare feet slapped against the cold floor.

"I bet she's been down here before." Pig felt a higher level of bravery and fright.

"We should've gone with her. Pig, it's our only chance to see if Mom's down here!"

"If we don't see her, it could mean that she's still alive!"

A low deep growl sent them galloping off behind Tina. "Okay, wait! Stop, listen." After turning another corner, Nina grabbed Pig by the arm. Slowing, they saw Tina disappearing down the hall, cutting another corner. "Listen. It stopped! Nothing's coming."

"If we're going to find Momma's remains, we have to check every room. Quick!" Pig said. She was even more aware of their brother being somewhere down there with them.

Gathering every inch of courage from within them, the two sisters toughened their weak guts, trying not to think about the gore that awaited. Without thinking, they began to yank on handles and open doors. Skimming through each room for any sign of their mother, they wound up on the other end of the hallway.

Passing rooms of wooden beds and cleaning devices, they stopped at a door that reminded them of a hospital. "I wonder what's behind these doors." Pig examined the door in front of them. The second one stood tall on an adjoining wall. "Looks weird. I've never seen a real hospital, but the doors look just like these in the pictures."

It was always funny to Nina how Pig and Tina always knew so many things. As far back as she could remember, they were usually stuck in the house together.

"Hey, would you two quit making so much noise! All of that slamming doors and bumping things! If Daddy did come down here, we couldn't even lie about it!" Tina suddenly appeared behind them.

"Couldn't find her, could you?" Nina looked past the attitude.

"No, I didn't finish checking the back area. I came here when I heard you two. I thought you were her! Now would you two cut it out and come on! If you're gonna be down here, you gotta stay close. We gotta hurry up and find her," Tina said.

"What's the plan? How can all this be under our house?" Receiving a suspicious look from Tina, Nina followed her big sister down the hall.

Traveling to the center of the floor, the three passed two rooms. As Nina peeked into an open window, Pig observed that the floor continued off into a black open area.

"More stairs. I can't believe it!" Nina's forehead and finger pressed up against the dusty glass window. "I'm not going down there. No more steps," Nina said as Pig pulled her away from the booth and toward the dark end of the enormous room.

"I can't see anything down here, Rashida!" Tina stubbed her toe on something hard. "There has to be a light down here."

Stepping on something gritty, Pig spotted what appeared to be a handle protruding from some sort of work table. Walking over to it, she picked up an industrial flashlight. "Does anything work around here?" She thumbed the small power button and knocked it against the palm of her hand three times. It flashed twice before emitting a steady beam of light.

"What the?" Tina saw small piles of what looked like human remains in the far corner.

"Momma?" Tears began to pour from Nina's eyes as she looked at the mess of human and animal body parts. Drowning in heartache, she knew that determining what was her mother's were now impossible. "We're never going to find her body!"

Already accepting her mother's death, Pig remained silent and cold on the inside. Only one thing was left to prove, but she dared not speak a word of it.

"That's it, Rashida!" Tina shouted at the top of her lungs. Looking at what appeared to be her sister mourning over the decomposed shattered bones of a dead woman, she reached over and pulled Pig and Nina away. "Stop it. She's not here!" She tried to calm Nina and grabbed her face. "Nina, stop crying! She's not down here." She got Nina's attention, slowing her falling tears. "I've known where she's been the whole time. I've been keeping it a secret from you two. Stop crying. Don't worry. I'll tell you about it, but let's find Rashida first and get out of here."

"I want to leave now." A creepy feeling crept up Pig's spine. "Let's leave her! She'll come out sooner or later."

"Pig, I just can't leave her down here like this! Why can't you two just go back by yourselves? I'll be okay!" Tina began to accept the consequences of her actions.

Nina grabbed Tina by the waist and looked up at her. "Tina, we're not leaving you either! Sisters stay together. Let's find her and go. Come on." Pig pulled her away as they all began to call out for Rashida.

"Rashida, come out! We're leaving. We have to go! Where is she?" Pig began to walk away with Nina.

"Come on. Let's hurry up and check the rooms again. She's gotta be hiding down here somewhere!"

Nina dashed ahead of her sisters. In a hurry to get back upstairs before her dad returned, she ran up to the double set of rooms, desperately twisting the doorknobs. Throwing her body against the doors, she attempted to force them open. Eyeing the closed door at the end of the long hallway, the quest to locate Rashida intensified.

One door had only holes where a handle should have been. It revealed a shadow of movement inside; a thick board of wood was wedged between two metal hoops, locking it from the outside.

"I found her!" Nina slid the board out of the door. "She's in here!" Without thinking, she swung open the door and looked back at her sisters, smiling confidently. Pig approached when she realized that she was beginning to walk awkwardly over a sudden crunching surface. A path of bones and food jabbed at her feet and stuck between her toes.

"Ew. Oh no—you found the door." Pig's knee's weakened and her legs turned to gel. "It's the monster!" She used her remaining energy to lift her arm and point.

With an old newspaper stuck to her leg, Nina returned her attention to the door. As Tina rush to Pig's aid, Nina's face transformed from confused to distraught. Turning as cold as ice, her heart plummeted to her feet and returned to a rhythm of wild tribal patterns. Every ounce of energy drained from her body at the sight of a towering figure in the corner.

A heavy series of grunts snorted from a misshaped hairy back upon two thick molds of massive legs. A humongous elbow flapped uneasily at the little girl. Cocking his head to the side, Junior turned around, showing a set of beady eyes—the same color as theirs—sunken into the sides of his deformed face. A frowning, meaty forehead and bushy brows hid the odd pupils above a smile of missing, rotting teeth. Extra baby teeth crowded hair that gruesomely extended over its entire body. A massive head perched between broad shoulders while the left arm rested by its side. Black curly hair surrounded the bulging chin, connecting to the smashed cranium. In the flesh, Junior stood feet away from the entrance.

Stumbling backward at the sight of his twisting face, Nina was disturbingly distracted by her brother's right arm and perverted moving hand. Two steps into her run, Nina stumbled to the floor again, and she broke into a backward crawl as a thick white substance flew by her face. When Junior stepped toward her, she cracked a mighty scream as Rashida quietly shut the door and locked it with a slab of wood.

"What are you girls doing down here?" Rashida asked.

Junior howled and pounded on the door. Scaring the three girls with every hit, they darted off in a frenzy of screams, pulling Rashida with them.

"Wait, stop! I can't go any further! Wait, why are we still running? He's in the room. It's just Junior; don't worry." Rashida hunched over to catch her breath inside the hall that led back upstairs. Throwing up along the bottom of the boarded wall, she wiped her mouth and looked at the three. "Now what were you girls doing down here by yourselves?"

"Miss Rashida, you ran off on us and everything! You got crazy this time; look at where we're at." Tina tried to explain as Nina and Pig walked by.

"Let's go; your Daddy, remember?"

A loud bang sent them all running upstairs.

For the next hour, Rashida and the girls made sure the old shabby house was in tip-top shape for Jamanny's approval. The floor was swept and scrubbed, the dinner table was set, and the walls were wiped well. Rashida was still feeling the negative effects of the drugs, but they completed their tasks. A new pot of spaghetti and meatballs waited to be eaten; a few dishes in the sink vibrated to the plinking of drips that fell from the rusty faucet. Lamond and Omack ran around the house as Rashida and the girls sat patiently at the table. Mr. Tiny, the dog, reminded them of the undiscovered world outside the house.

Nina looked around the table at her sisters; they also had their heads down. Tina showed no signs of life with her head down. Rashida was starring down at her plate, crying and dying slowly. She yawned and said, "I'm tired."

"Me too. I'm ready for bed," Pig replied.

"I'm ready to get my butt whooped or go to sleep. I wonder where they are. They should have been here by now," Tina said.

"Jamanny … I'm so sick and tired of hearing that Godforsaken name in this house!" Rashida's face turned into a ravenous snarl as she stared at her plate. "Spare me!" She smacked the dish away. "One day, Tina, you're gonna have to take my place and be the woman of this house—and one day you two will take her place."

"Rashida, come on. I don't want to hear that! I don't want to be the woman of this funky house!"

"Me either, I hate it here!"

"Good. That's my girls. Promise me—no, promise yourselves—that one day, you'll get far away from here. This ain't no place for a woman or to raise kids. Jamanny ain't no kind of damn father! He wants slaves and puppets. If you don't find a way outta here, that man and those boys are going to kill you." Rashida suddenly started making sense. As if she was trying to focus on what she was trying to say, her eyelids blinked to the tapping of her finger against the table.

"Why do you let him hit you?" Pig slid her head off the table and raised it just high enough to view her devious eyes.

"Pig!" Tina said.

"No baby, it's okay. I think it's time for us to talk, Rashida said. "I think we need to talk." She sat back in a deep sweat, taking a long swallow. "My eyes were once closed, but today they're open. The devil has kept me a prisoner for many years now, in my own house, but today will be different." She closed her eyes and slowly rocked in place. "Never again shall I fear …"

"Miss Rashida!" Nina sighed as the woman drifted off. "She's gone. Did she take more drugs?"

"Where's our mother, Miss Rashida?" Pig slapped the table, awakening Rashida.

"I said I would tell you two! What's wrong with you?" Tina yelled.

Rashida laughed out loud. "I did love him. Then she came and took him away from me. She was so beautiful. She slayed the demon and freed me. Now all that remains is the devil and the monster. Her eyes …" She stared at Nina. "Her eyes were so unholy, but divine. The goose will come looking for her golden egg. And today I'll get my laugh. Never again shall I fear, never again will I feel pain. Gotta run or fight until the death of your soul." She barely stood, leaving the table. "Today will be different, I'll get my laugh." She staggered away. "I'm going to lie down. Wake me when the dogs get in."

"What? That's it? She didn't even tell us anything! More riddles." Pig said as they watched Rashida leave.

"Wake me when the dogs get in? What does she? Oh shoot; I forgot about Tiny!" Nina jumped up and left the room as well. Picking up a small collection of her father's clothes, Nina opened the front door. Tiger squeezed by and ran outside as Tausha, a young girl seeing her brother, Dozer, knocked into the wind.

"Hi, is Dozer in?" Tausha's grin fit into a warm, gentle face.

"No, but he should be back at any time. I have to go!" Nina abruptly ran off to the back of the house where the dog was kept. Alongside a path that led to a field, she walked up to the tree by the fence that separated the property from the woods and nearby creek. Growling and barking slightly caught her off guard. Tossing down the clothes, she bravely walked up to Tiny and unchained him from the tree. Transferring light energy with brute force, the canine pulled her along happily through a broken section of the fence into the woods.

It had begun to get dark when Jamanny and his two sons arrived in different clothing. They entered the house as if they hadn't previously killed and buried anyone. "Where's my supper?" Jamanny asked, checking the table for all the children. His eyes slid toward Tausha.

"It's in the oven." Tina said, watching his body language become aggressive.

"Doza, you better handle that before I do. You know the rules; its supper time. " Jamanny pointed at the young lady's face. "Where's Rashida?"

"Upstairs," Nina said.

"See ... y'all done got into some shit; y'all done something! Hold on; wait until I get back in here! G'on get them plates made!" Jamanny said before walking into his room. "There's my favorite son." Jamanny rubbed Lamond's head as he ran by Dozer and Timothy. "Give me a plate for your brother!"

"He's not going to let me stay, is he?" Tausha stood and smiled at Dozer.

"You have to leave, Tausha. Go ahead! We'll talk later." Dozer escorted her toward the door, but she kept finding reasons to stay.

Returning from giving Junior his meal, Jamanny entered the hall and stepped on a crumpled page of a newspaper. Reading it and checking its date, he recognized it as belonging in the basement. Crumbling the page, he tossed it into the darkness of the hall. With all assumptions toward learning already pointed at Dozer, his bristling white brows lowered and curled into the shape of an anchor. Tightening his lips, he slowly walked back toward the living room. Stomping through the kitchen, the tall figure of a wild haired man stepped to the table and sat without saying a word. "Woman, get yo butt down here right now!"

Feeling the heavy tension rising inside the room, Nina and Pig began to stuff their mouths with food—in case anything happened, they would have full stomachs. Tina pecked and pinched off her plate while the boys engulfed noodles and sauce.

"Did you take care of the gal, boy?" Jamanny bellowed.

Dozer took a bite of bread, looked up, and said, "Yes."

"I don't want you getting wrapped up in that, is that clear? From the looks of her, I can tell she opens her legs for anybody. Rashida! Damn it, I said get down here, woman!" Jamanny yelled. Rolling the red noodles around his fork, he placed the food in his mouth.

"Actually, she's not like that at all, Dad. I wanted to know if I could hang out with her and a couple of guys this weekend?" Dozer dropped his head and began eating.

"Did you say actually?" Jamanny said. "And did you say a couple of guys?" Snickering out particles of spaghetti, he choked up his food, spit it in a napkin, wiped his mouth, and held it in his hand. "So you mean to tell me, Doza Durgen, that you have friends out there?" He pointed a long scaly finger to the door as Dozer nodded. "Oh, you happy about that, boy? We happy, are we? It appears to me that someone in this house has been learnin' and doing an awful lot of reading. Just when I was trying to have a decent supper! Rashida, let's go! It seems like the only one who appreciates me around here is Tiger! Where is Tiger? Anybody seen Tiger?" He checked under the table for any sign of his cat. "Rashida!"

"Stop yelling! I'm coming." Rashida shuffled downstairs and found her place at the table across from Jamanny. "So how's the food, Manny?" Staring at him coldly, she asked him for something that she never asked for before: his opinion.

"The food?" He lifted his head from over his plate. "I was just telling these little bastards how delicious it was, bitch! Now what ya do to it—and where's my goddamn cat? These shriveled up pieces of meat better not be Tiger! And why does it smell so funny?" He sifted through the meal with his fork, spotting two strands of what he considered to be fur or hair. Not noticing his daughters holding back their laughter, he watched a few baby roaches scouring for scraps, not touching the food that had been spilled onto the table. "You better start talkin'!" Jamanny pointed his fork at Rashida.

"Aww, what's wrong? You don't like it?" Rashida broke into a loud laugh.

"What the hell? Woman, have you been in my—"

Jamanny leaned over the table and looked closely at Rashida's pupils and behavior. Along the table's edge, discretely balancing a meatball on his towering fork, he flicked the utensil directly into a mouse hole along the wall. While the family continued to pretend to dig into their plates, Jamanny gazed at Timothy's clueless expression, Dozer's stone face, and then the girls' foolish grins. "Nina, you been teachin' that dog with y'all clothes like I taught you?"

He accepted her nod as a sudden symphony of odd ill squeals turned their heads to the direction of the mouse hole. Jamanny's mouth dropped and hung open as a rodent ran between the table and wall, spiraling into a sliding spin. Smacking its head and body violently against the floor in a bloody fit, the small rat foamed at the mouth and fell flat. Its tail nervously twitched, but it refused to die. Taking a hard swallow, Jamanny wiped the back of his neck with his hand.

"Don't worry, Manny. I put in your favorite ingredient." Rashida said. "Pussy, meow! Don't you like pussy? You live nine extra lives." Her words and wicked laughter sent him spitting the food onto the floor.

"You evil wench!" Jamanny lunged at Rashida and felt a cold jagged blade around his neck. Having unconsciously caught her hand, he checked his lightly bleeding neck with the other and smacked her to the floor. "I don't believe this shit!" He grabbed her by the hair, took his nearby rifle, and pressed it against Dozer's nose. "Really? Is it gonna be like this seriously? Out of everything I've done for this family! Everybody up! Bring yo ass and leave them goddamn babies here!" He shouted at his daughters, "Take her to the fuckin' red room!"

"What we do, Daddy? Come on, Miss Rashida. Dad?" Dozer asked as his father tossed him twice.

"Timothy, the red room. Jamanny twisted his large fingers into Rashida's hair and slid her small body across the floor into the wall. "And I do mean bring your ass straight back here to the car! No funny business, boy; you got two minutes."

Timothy felt Rashida up before dragging her off deep within the house—never to be seen or heard from again.

Under the heavy hail of curse words and hits, Jamanny forced his children into his trusty old van. Under the gun, he sat them down. He tossed the shovels into the vehicle with them. Then, jumping inside, he tapped Dozer on the shoulder with the gun and tossed him the keys. Slinging mud behind them, the van sped off, leaving Lamond and Omack behind.

As rain exploded across the van, Nina thought of Rashida, her words, and her mother. Realizing that her father was really a madman, tears began to fall at the thought of running away. Having never been outside the property on her own, their location was unrecognizable to Nina or any of the girls.

Scared of what her father was going to do next, Tina shook her head at Timothy's ridiculous smirk. "We're all crazy," she mumbled.

Driving deep into the property, miles away from the backyard, just beyond the field of wild horses, the vehicle came to a halt. The passenger door opened as a large dirty boot stepped out into the muddy grass. "Out, and ya betta step out with ya shovels in hand!" Jamanny stood over his seedlings, watching them exit in single file.

Feeling a strong force shove her head forward, Nina collided with Pig and joined her in carrying the tools over the field of flowers and weeds. Between a rough of bushes, something of thorny nature scratched her ankles and feet. Entering a familiar area, Nina thought of how the ground looked the same behind their house.

In the field, things appeared not to grow so well. Jamanny took them near a flat section under the moonlight. Tossing Timothy a flashlight, Jamanny revealed eerie openings in the ground.

Jamanny's chest stuck out like a drill sergeant; his face resembled a vampire under the light. "I have put everything into this family and into everything ours. That's right ... ours. When I'm dead and gone, everything I own and possess will be yours. I've told you long and dreadful stories of what I've been through. Some of you have even seen the evils of the world come after me with your own eyes! I have defeated them all, each, one by one, all by myself, one after the other." His eyes bulged below his meaty forehead. Looking at Dozer and Timothy, he pointed to Pig and bent down. "But the funny thing is, despite how much you know and I tell you, some of you still choose to go against me." Grabbing the corner of a tarp, Jamanny pulled back a large fold of material from the ground. "When you go against my words, do the plum opposite of what I say, try to kill me, and disturb the rules of my happy quiet home, that, children, is the same thing as giving me a slow death! And I can't have that! I raised you, each of you! Bedded and clothed your little filthy stankin' butts! Provided food and a roof up over your heads!" The children stood in a straight line as he dropped the tarp and paced. "Out there ain't the place for you; you wasn't even raised out there! You can dream all you want and even attempt to leave my house, but let me tell you something: ain't nobody breaking up my family, and ain't nobody who's done that living." He grabbed another side of the large tarp.

Drenched and beginning to shiver in the chilled night air, the five kids watched in silence; their father unpeel eight pre-started plots of graves. The one that was the scariest was the size of a rhino, which they knew could only be for Junior. The two smallest ones were the same lengths of Lamond and Omack's small bodies.

"This right here is your future. Now stand beside the one you feel is your future destination, and don't make me send you on an early trip. I carries a mean time machine!" He held up his rifle and smiled at them following his instructions precisely. "Now, if I ever catch, no—whenever you make your mind up to leave this family, or go out to make some friends, or bring some of that good old outside learnin' and readin' in with ya, I will kill you. Any questions?"

He loaded his rifle and prepared to shoot the first child that spoke. "Now here's what we gonna do—we're gonna climb down into these here holes and work on our futures. That means, make it a bigger and a brighter place. Now get to digging! See here, you are miles and miles away from civilization—and ain't nobody gonna come looking for your body. In this place, it's what I say goes; I make the rules! I am the governor and the president! The only law I obey is my own; hell, I am the law."

He took a sheriff's badge from the inside of his pocket, flipped it into the air, and blasted it into the dampness of the night. "We may be in the United States, but this is the State of Jamanny!"

He swiped Dozer across the back, sending him toppling into the grave as lightning and thunder filled the sky.

Chapter 6:
A JOURNEY'S END

———— ✳ ————

In the unknown, wild terrain of Mississippi, a black car kicked up dirt and sand. "I can't believe you came … and we're here." Faith turned a map up and down, reading it.

"I can't believe you asked for a car and don't know how to drive! And wait, how do you know we're here?" Julia came to a screeching halt as a stray cow meandered across the road with a rope around its neck. It was branded with the letters JD. "Okay, this is getting weird." She swerved around the animal. "Hey, when we find this guy, you come from the front, and I'll come from the back. It'll be a surprise attack."

"Jay, I'm glad you came along." Looking at her old almost forgotten friend, Faith suddenly remembered the time when Julia drove her around.

"Come on. Who else does Destiny have? You don't remember your friends because you really didn't have any—just like me. Your girl Nodia moved to another state, and the only other friends you had were Kashonda and Passion—and they died in the crash. Since then, it's been all downhill for me. I've been praying for you every day and waiting." Julia pushed her sunglasses further on her pale nose. "We just happen to—years later—be at the same place at the same time, and you tell me that some old man may have Destiny in his house. I used to keep her every day. She was like a niece. I had to come! My life is nothing now." She wiped the corner of her eye. "I'm glad I could help."

Upon a dirt road in the countryside, Mary Rae Anna's company car pulled up beside a row of old houses. An old black man in tattered clothes stepped away from a barrel of fire; a black woman with funny hair and city clothes stepped out of the car and slowly approached him.

"Howdy," Faith said to the elderly fellow as he stared her up and down.

"You gals aren't from around here; are you?" His rusty voice squeaked and cracked.

In jumpsuit pants and a muscle shirt, Faith took off a black fingerless motorcycle glove. "You could say that." She looked him up and down to assure that he wasn't a threat. "I'm lost, and I'm trying to get here. I don't see any signs." She moved closer to the man and showed him an address on a small piece of paper.

"You're in the country, sweetie. They're not too fond of signs around these parts." The man's hand began to tremble. Pushing the paper away, he wiped his balding head with a dingy cloth. "It's just right up the street there, but why on earth would you want to go there? Don't you know it's all empty around town? Nobody lives here no more."

Faith looked at him oddly as Julia moved the car closer. "What happened to all the people? You're still here."

"I ain't got nothing else I suppose. I ain't nobody—just an old man living off the land. As for the people who lived here, they all died off, moved out, or got bought out of house and land. You on private property now, acres and acres of it. So you gonna have to be careful. Hot dang, y'all some purty dames!" The old man smiled a set of black gums and sat a piece of a chicken leg down on a napkin.

"Aw thank you. That's mighty sweet of you." Faith patted his arm. "We're looking for someone."

Licking his fingers, the man smacked his mouth and wiped his hands on his pants. "Like I said, this is private property. If I were you, I wouldn't go down too far. Some folks tend to get a little funny when it comes to they own land around here. That's how it is in some parts of Mississippi, ya know?"

"How far is too far?"

"Well, it's all pretty much abandoned and lonely around here. Now if you go too far down yonder, then you'll be running into old Mr.

Durgen's place somewhere down there. He's the owner of most of these parts, but he ain't normally around. But you ain't gotta be worried about seeing him; you have to be more concerned about him seeing you first. He ain't too friendly and don't take too kindly to city folk at all."

"Thank you. That's all I need to know. Much obliged, old timer." Faith put her glove back on and turned her back on the man as he continued talking.

"Hey, how can I turn down a beautiful face like that? I scratch your back if you scratch mine! Ha, ha, ha! So who you say you lookin' for? Nobody has visited here in ages. Whew, they're tough," the old man said before he was engulfed in a cloud of dust as the two women sped off.

A half a mile from where they saw the homeless man, Julia stopped the car. "Did you hear him?"

"Yep, old man Durgen. He said it." Faith stared off in a daze, becoming more amped, the more she thought of her daughter. "We're right here, baby, close. I can feel you." She began to pray that her child was still alive.

"We're on the right path, Faith. This is it." Julia glanced over at her best friend whose child she had helped deliver. "We came all this way. Do you really want to do this?"

"It's now or never, Jay. My one and only chance at doing something— and saving my daughter. There's no other way. Do or die." Faith looked down at the shotgun she had dug up at the old house. Placing her hand over it, she remembered when her grandmother had used it to save her life. She thought of how she would use it to save her daughter.

Chapter 7:
THE RISE OF DOZER

———— ❋ ————

❚❚This is delicious, Mr. Durgen. Did that sweet old Miss Rashida make
it? You know she was really nice. I like her. Whatever happened to
her?"

Tausha was eating a plate of fried catfish, mashed potatoes, and
peas. She was in love with the boy; her surprise visit and brave persistent
talking had landed her a spot at the Durgen family's dining room table.
The perky spirit that had gotten her through the door had fallen victim
to cold stares, obnoxious table manners, and constant groaning from
Jamanny.

Jamanny's glassy eyes shifted between Dozer and Tausha. Hating the
sight of strangers and anyone besides his family in his home, he cringed
at the mere sound of the uppity, high-pitched voice. Not answering her
questions or responding to any of her comments, his blood thickened,
and his veins began to sprout along his temples.

Dozer had let her talk him into letting her sit at the table. He looked
at his plate the whole time, occasionally bumping Tausha's leg, signaling
her to tone it down.

"What?" Tausha began to grow agitated by his father's attitude.
When she couldn't hold back the her emotions any longer, she said,
"Okay, Mr. Durgen. Look, Dozer, I'm sorry." She placed her hand on
Dozer's shoulder. "Mr. Durgen, I have feelings for your son, and I am
trying to be a respectful woman and bring myself to your attention

because I am in his life! I've done everything to befriend you and try to get you to like me."

"Tausha, please." Dozer tried to calm her down, but she slapped his hands away.

"No, Dozer! See, I just want to know how come your dad doesn't like me? I like him." Tausha wiped her mouth and tossed her napkin over her plate. "I don't understand, Mr. Durgen, I've been talking to you nicely and with respect this whole time, but you haven't said nothing."

Still not responding, another slow spoonful ended Jamanny's meal. Sliding the plate to the side, Tina immediately got up from the table and removed his plate, replacing it with a bottle of beer. Without a bottle opener, his hand easily popped the lid. While the others finished their meal, he drained half the beer. Taking two pills, he turned back to Tausha.

"I do nothing but good for him!" Tausha said. "We talk about everything—the future, how things work in the world. Did you know that your son couldn't read? Well, he can now. I've been helping him learn everything that he should know at his age!" She smacked the table. "I know he's your son, and I'm not trying to change or come between that! I respect you, but your son can read thanks to me. For Pete's sake, Mr. Durgen! He can read! I know you don't like me, but all I'm trying to say is that I really care for your son. I'm not leading him down the wrong path. I'm not a bad person, and I'm not going anywhere."

"So you ain't going nowhere, huh? And you say you're the one responsible for teachin' my boy these worldly things?" Jamanny finished his beer, sat upright, and belched loudly over the table.

"Nope, I'm not going anywhere, Mr. Durgen. I'm going to always treat him right and be in his life. I love him." Feeling a small hint of progress, Tausha blushed slightly. Paying no attention to the siblings clearing the table, she watched Jamanny slowly turn to the love of her life.

"And you love him?" Scooting away from the table, Jamanny looked at Dozer with a cold face. "Take this wench to the red room, boy."

"Dad, no! Come on, Dad. Please?"

"Who is he calling a wench? And I'm not going to nobody's room! Who is he?" Tausha sat up in her chair. "Are you going to let him talk to me like that?"

"Take her ass to the muthafuckin' red room before I send you with her!" Jamanny's arm stretched over the table, sending the beer bottle slicing across Dozer's forehead, exploding against the wall like a missile.

"Dad!" Dozer cried and smacked his head. "Come on, Dad, please! I like her! Don't make me do this!" He stood in tears and blood.

"Dozer, are you okay? Oh my GOD, you are a goddamn crazy person! Why did you do that?" Tausha screamed, noticing all the family members standing in the far corners of the room. Seeing the blood from Dozer's head, she covered her mouth in fright.

"Do I need to go to my room, boy? Am I really gone need to do that? Take her."

"Take her what? Wait, I'm not going anywhere!" Tausha started checking for her things.

With nothing but perverted thoughts, Timothy stepped from in front of Omack and Lamond to assist his brother as Jamanny snatched Tina's plate. "You step yo ass over here, son, and I swear, I swear I'll beat your head to the white meat with this good china!" As catfish bones tumbled to the floor, Timothy stepped back.

"Sorry, Tausha." Tears mixed with Dozer's blood as he stood over her.

"No, you don't have to apologize for this! It's your choice to listen to this crap or not!" She pointed to his father. "If it's over, it's over. Your choice, your loss. You're not trying to be a real man anyway!" She slung her purse over her shoulder. Hurt that he wouldn't stand up with her, she stood up, leaned, and in a flash of light, fell to the floor in horrific screams and gurgles. Dozer hit her with a fury of punches. Kicking for freedom, she unblocked her face slightly to see a chair coming down upon her. She was dragged away and never seen again.

Inhaling and exhaling loudly, Jamanny unbuckled his pants and took a seat at the table. "Tina, fix me another plate." He lit a fat cigar and smiled wickedly at Nina and Pig. Sitting back, his giggle faded into a choke of coughs and thick smoke.

Weeks of tyranny came and went as another new day dawned in the house. Upstairs remained quiet in the morning; the oldest boys were missing from their beds. Their messy rooms told of their last encounter. Singing birds scattered as the nonstop barking of Tiny opened Nina's eyes. A sound from downstairs made her flinch. On the floor, at the foot of the closet, a small spider crawled over her left hand and onto the floor. It continued under her brother's bed.

Jamanny smacked his dry mouth and frowned at the sudden sound of the dog. "Stupid mutt. Nina, shit!" He roughly wiped his face and sighed wearily. Deciding to shut the dog up himself, he sat up in the chair. He had puffy bags under his eyes. A slight headache from a night of alcohol and pills pounded against his temple as he wobbled about.

Having slept in the chair, he attempted to straighten his stiff neck and back. The continuous barking intensified the pain in his head. He called for the oldest sons, but got no response. He walked past an open window and yelled, "Shut your dang trap, Tiny! Quiet!"

He hurried to the front door. Wiping his mouth, he prepared for the unwanted brightness of the sun. Unlocking the door, he placed his hand upon the cool handle and pulled. "Didn't I say shut the hell—"

The light of the sky blurred his sight as his sentence was stopped by a fist colliding into his chin, snapping into his throat. His cheekbones were crushed by a small brick that was wielded by an unseen force from outside. Grabbing his face and holding his neck, he staggered back into the house. "What the fuck?"

A board slammed across the midsection. A woman with dreads stood before him. A bright flash and the sound of thunder rumbled through the house as the old man fell back into his favorite chair.

"Where's my goddamn daughter, you son of a bitch?" Faith pointed the barrel of a smoking shotgun directly at his wretched soul. Faith grinned at the sight of his dripping blood.

In shock for the first time in a long time, her thirst for revenge sent his heart beating. Grabbing his chest, he leaned back against the seat. Groaning in surprise and fear, a tear trickled from one eye. The children ran around upstairs. The sight of the gun being brought closer to his face indicated that his end had finally drawn near.

"What's happening?" Tina ran into the hall as Timothy burst out of the room behind her.

"No. You know the routine!" Timothy grabbed her by the arm as the sisters came out of their rooms.

"What was that? We heard a gun." Nina tried to dash down the stairs, but Timothy blocked her.

"Not until Pops says it's clear! So get on in there right now! You too. Go on back in the room!" Timothy straightened up his clothes. The girls stood and still did not budge in front of him, listening from the top of the staircase.

"I'm going to ask you one last time. If you don't answer, I promise on my little girl's life that your head is going to fucking explode into little pretty itty bitty shapes and colors! Now where is my baby? What did you do with her?" Faith's jittery finger held the trigger, aiming at the leathery mug of the tall old man. Her face, twitching of rage and hate, burned with the desire to kill him. The countdown from three convinced her to continue the search without him.

In a twist, Jamanny grabbed the shotgun, pulled Faith toward him with brute strength, and uncontrollably fired past her head into the far wall. In a vicious game of tug of war, she stomped on his leg, nearly breaking it. Ripping the weapon free from his clutches, she clubbed him several times across the shoulders and head.

"Destiny!" she shouted as a mighty boot kicked the gun from her grip. Rushing her, they both fell over the coffee table, breaking it apart. Wrestling on top of her, Jamanny tried to take control of her wildly swinging hands. Drawing his mighty arm back to pulverize her, Faith sent him diving sideways after stabbing him between the ribs with a jagged piece of table and nail.

The living room shelf fell over them as he rose through the rolling, falling, and breaking ornaments. Leaping over the couch, Faith aimed the weapon at the center of his chest, and her finger curled over the trigger. In a flash of intense light, Faith's body dropped numbly to the floor in a thud.

Behind her, Dozer breathed harshly with a wrench in his hand. In the narrow kitchen, Julia was unconscious, stretching out loosely as if she were making snow angels on the floor. Dragging her in, he stopped and glanced at his father's face. Faith's lower end collapsed against the floor.

Chapter 8:
THE BAD HOUSE, PART 2

———— ✳ ————

A pair of dark brown eyes opened to the view of a slowing, spinning, dim, flickering light that danced across an old surface. Reminding her of the reflection of water alongside a pool at night, Faith gradually gathered her thoughts and tried to move. A pain in the back of her pounding head forced her neck to relax.

Exhausted, dazed and weak, she made out various pipes and cracked, bubbling paint on the ceiling. Rolling her head, her joints and neck began to itch as she released a scream. She was bound and locked in some sort of small room. She frantically snapped at the rope, attempting to bend a limb enough to free herself. Her body fell flat against the hard bed. Faith looked down at her feet. In the corner, the light intensified toward the floor. A candle burned nearby. Sections of the four walls were torn and busted, revealing large empty spaces.

She screamed into the blackness. "Where are you? Where's my baby?" The sound of whisper through the wall caught her ear. Tolerating the throbbing pain in her head, she eyed a door with a window a few feet from the bed.

"Rashida?" A high-pitched voice of a young woman crawled out of the shadows. "Is that you? Get me out of here! I'm sorry, tell them I'm sorry." The woman wept loudly.

Faith considered responding. "I'm not your friend! I'm not Rashida. I'm looking for someone. Where are we?" She slowed her breathing to listen better. "Where are we?"

The woman coughed. "Somewhere under the fuckin' house!" Her voice faded into groans of pain. "I don't wanna die in here!"

Hearing the possibility that she was still close to her child, Faith quickly gained as much information as she could. "Is there a way out of here?" She tried to raise her arm to her mouth to chew through the ropes, but she failed.

"They keep you locked up and torture you every day. You never see daylight." The sound of vomiting turned Faith's head in the opposite direction.

"Have you seen a little girl?" Faith looked around for any sharp object. "I'm looking for my daughter." She took another rest, listened, and thought about Julia and her next move.

"I dunno. This house is full of little girls." The grim voice paused between sounds of falling bits of drywall. "I don't remember how many, but the father controls them all. He's evil! He made his son do this to me. They're going to do this to you too!" She faded into a frenzy of sick whimpers, moans, and coughs.

"Is that talking? Are you communicating now?" Jamanny yelled. "Put her back in there. Get her!"

A woman's cries bellowed from the darkness.

"No, let me go! I'm sorry. No, not in there!" The woman's nails scraped the wall past Faith's door. "Let me go! No, you get out of here! They're going to kill us!" She was being dragged down the hall. "I'm Tausha! My name is Tausha!"

Faith's sensed danger; the scene caused her to realize the severity of the situation. She pulled at the ropes with all her might and arched her body. "Let us go! You worthless son of a bitch! All you're doing is hurting helpless women, you chicken shit! You're weak! Why don't you be a man for the first time, Jamanny? Or are you afraid of dying like your son, Jamondo?"

"Who is that talking shit? Oh you talking real big in there tied to my bed, young lady! Don't you get them panties all in a bunch now, because I already done took them off ya! Now your ass is next!" Under the thickest eyebrows Faith had ever seen, familiar eyes peered in through the dirty window.

"Fuck you!" Faith snapped as the ropes started to burn marks into her wrist and ankles.

"No, you're the one who's about to get fucked." The tall man unlocked the door and opened it. With the appearance of a tired old farmer just coming out of a field, he shuffled his muddy boots across the floor.

Noticing his victim sizing him up, he leaned his slim body upright, displaying defined muscles. With no shirt, dark jean overalls, bandages, and a sling, Jamanny eased beside the bed and touched Faith's face. As she pulled away, he held onto a thick strand of dreadlocks and pulled them out of her head. "How long do you think you've been here? You know, you're quite a resilient one. I pumped you up with enough tranquilizers to lay down an elephant for ten months, yet you still wake up smiling, full of energy. I like that."

"Where's Destiny? Where's my baby?" Faith watched him close the door and pace the bed.

"You know … when you came, I wasn't sure who the hell you were, but when you held that awfully familiar piece of steel right between my eyes, which by the way, belongs to my deceased and beloved queen, I knew exactly who you were. Guns are powerful! Did you know that I also had one pointed at my face like a kazillion times—even used on me, how ironic?" He slapped his leg and shook his head laughing. "As for your daughter, Destiny, there is no Destiny. Consider her a dream, a memory, that you can only see when you close your eyes." He walked back to the door.

"I'll kill you, you bastard! I'm going to rip your fuckin' heart out and gut you like a fish!" Faith screamed and kicked furiously as the visions of her daughter and family dying in vain brought tears to her eyes.

"Doza, Timothy, get your butts in here! Doza!" Jamanny called. "Hey boy, get your ass in here right now!" He pointed to the floor.

"Yeah, Pops? Whatcha screaming for? We can hear ya all over the planet. We had to make sure she was right!" Timothy was grinning from ear to ear. "What next? Oh her. I been waitin' to get me one like that. Bet she smells good too!" He howled and touched his belt anxiously as Jamanny shoved him away with one hand. "I been wantin' her!"

"Boy, stand yo happy go lucky ass still right here next to me! Doza, go on in there and put something in her mind so she can remember us."

He stepped to the side as his son stared at him blankly. "Go ahead, boy. This'll be good for ya! It'll take your mind right off that gal."

"I don't want to." Dozer thought of Tausha and how much he cared for her. Knowing that his father could blow his top, depending on what he said, he cleaned up the meaning behind the words. "I told you I don't like them types." He glanced at his dirty clothes to hide his watering eyes.

"Types?" Jamanny burst into a wicked laughter and dug into his pocket, retrieving his pill bottle. "Timothy, do you hear this stuff? Boy, you don't got no type! Now get in there and do your business! Get her done!" He poked Dozer in the chest. "Come on now. Quit actin' like it's your first time! I need you to go in there and do like I say, boy!" Jamanny placed a hand on the back of Dozer's neck and pushed him into the room with Faith. "Go teach her a lesson. Show her what you're made of."

"Dad, no! I don't want to do this. I don't like her! This is wrong. I can't get off on her! Why do you keep making me do this? She stinks!"

"Doza! Do what you're told. Don't make me bring the heat out on your backside, boy. Now enough talk—this ain't no family movie! Do it. Fuck her!"

"Sounds like you ain't running shit!" Faith smirked at Jamanny.

"Shut the hell up! That's all right; I'll learn the both of ya. Timothy, find my bat, son!" Jamanny popped his tablets. "Negro, you got three seconds to fuck her brains out or else yo ass is grass." His smile fell and his temples filled with bulging veins again.

"But she's old, and she's ugly?" Dozer yelled.

"Boy, she's younger than that thing we had sitting around here. You was poking her for years and years! No more talk, boy. Get in it!"

"I hate this house! You make me do everything!" Dozer jumped on the bed in a mad rage. "She's ugly. I hate her!" He spit on Faith and whaled on her face as Jamanny ran in to pull him off.

Not able to block the fierce punches of the troubled son, Faith leaned her head to one side to absorb most of the blows. After Dozer broke her jaw, he leaped off of her and fled the room, knocking Jamanny and his brother out the way.

Faith awakened to long, unsanitary wires being inserted through one side of her gums. She jerked and screamed from the unbearable pain. Relieved that the attack was over, she trembled with her face covered in blood and tears. Timothy started taping her head to a chair while Dozer pried her mouth open with his bare hands, packing it with cotton. Trying her best to squirm out of their clutches, she struggled to see over the swollen tissue around her eyes. "What the hell are you doing? Let me go!" Unable to close her mouth, she cursed them all as an unwanted mug appeared directly in front of her.

"Hello, beautiful." Jamanny placed a stack of towels on her lap. "Well, you were beautiful until my boy here gave you the knuckle sandwich." He laughed and continued to ignore Faith's mumble of foul threats and jokes. "Huh? What am I doing with you? I'm fixin' to help you out!" Jamanny pretended to understand her. "Apparently, as you might have noticed, by the way you pronounce those mighty fine syllables, your jaw is broken." He stretched a pair of latex gloves over his hands. When he started wiggling her hanging jaw, Faith jumped in pain. "Ouch, yep, it's broken all right. See, I'm the only friend you've got right now."

"Fuck you." Faith rolled her tongue, flinging blood and mucus on his face.

"Now should you really have done that, considering I have the upper hand right now?" He wiped his face and punched her in the stomach, knocking the wind out of her. "See, I'm all you got right now." He held her face still. "I was a little hurt and jealous at first when you got your back tooth knocked out because I wanted to do it! But, I got a plan. First I'm gonna heal you up real good, and then I'm going to personally break your jaw all over again." He laughed, setting a thin coil of wire on top of the towels. "I'm sorry we don't have Novocain or anesthesia in this here clinic so this is going to hurt just a bit. Heck, I guess that's why they call it torture." He held up a drill and turned it on. "Put the block in her mouth—and keep her nice and straight!" He went on with the heinous surgery of wiring her mouth.

Kicking and screaming for GOD's mercy, Faith filled the room with relentless cries of agony. A long slit was made on the side of her mouth as the skin's elasticity was tested by inexperienced hands. Squeezing out tears, she saw Jamanny smoking a cigar while pressing the drill through her jawbone.

Faith struggled to move. Managing to bust Dozer's lip with a quick head-butt, Jamanny nearly broke her neck as he shoved the drill into her mouth from the side of her head. Clenching every muscle, Faith's insides rattled and quaked from the action of the drill. Blood and flesh squirted over Jamanny's head and shoulders. Tremendous migraines shot throughout her head and face. Letting out a piercing shrill, her hands and legs clenched the wooden chair as it began to pop and crack under the pressure of the squeeze. Shaking, her eyes rolled back, and her body went into a state of shock. Her vision faded; Jamanny's eyes were the last thing she saw.

For weeks, Faith was abused and held captive. Refusing to eat, she was drugged and force-fed gruel and a collection of Jamanny's homemade mush. Emotionally defeated, with her unhealed mouth wired closed, Faith stared at two corners of the room. She listened to the faint sounds of children that seeped out of the hollow vents that ran throughout the entire structure. Hoping that one of the children was Destiny, her lips curled. She continued her daily project of picking at the fibers of the shaggy ropes that tied her to the bed. Decorated in bruises, handprints, and black eyes, she heard a movement outside the door. She prepared for another one of the old man's beatings for something ridiculous. Fanning away the tiny threads with her fingers, she relaxed the tension in her body to soothe the electrifying pain in her head and mouth.

"Rise and shine, my little pussycat." Jamanny peeped into the window of the door and opened it with a long squeak. In a drunken state, he staggered into the room, cutting an apple into sections with a small knife. Pulling up a chair from along the wall, he positioned it in front of the bed. "How ya feeling? I was just in the neighborhood and wanted to see if you needed anything—a piss, a shit? Whatever, you name it!" He glanced lustfully at her body in the candlelight. Smiling at how her legs were arched, streams of fluids gathered in her crotch, streaming off the edge of the table and down its legs.

"Humph," Jamanny said. "Still feisty, I see. That's okay, I like it wet. Mmmm." He licked his small lips and sat the apple in the chair. Shutting the door, he turned around to the sound of Faith passing gas.

"It doesn't matter what you do or how you smell. This is my house, and you're gonna please me." He unbuttoned his suspenders, dropping his overalls.

Faith watched him step out of his clothing. *Oh, hell no!* She thought as he lifted her shirt and licked her vagina. Picturing his foul mouth and horrible teeth, she became nauseated. Her shirt flipped above her breast.

Climbing onto the bed, Jamanny tumbled over her and began to suck her nipples. Across her neck and down her chest, he repeated the action before returning between her legs. Inserting two fingers, he sodomized her for the first time, trustfully untying her legs and folding them to his liking. Over her, he inserted his uncircumcised penis deep into her tight hole.

In disgust and pain, Faith took the abuse for thirty minutes, thinking of nothing but the perfect time to strike her revenge. As the table shook and rocked with Jamanny's sweat, heavy breathing, and grunts, he lifted up over her on his knees. In a cloud of climax and sounds of snapping rope, a swift hard poke in the eyes sent him flying off the bed. Sliding to her feet, Faith grabbed the knife near the apple, and stabbed Jamanny through his left testicle, piercing his inner thigh.

Jamanny hollered in a drunken rage as she ran out the room and locked the door. Unsure of where to go, she raced down the rectangular spiral of halls until she found the staircase. Extremely hurt and tired, she hurried to the top, passing an odd door with a stained window. The shadow of someone inside startled her and convinced her to move extra stealthily.

Further up the stairs, the sounds of children became clearer. Remembering to go through a narrow corridor, she entered Jamanny's closet, breaking through the wooden board that covered the entrance. Crawling toward a small light, she opened the closet door, knocking it against the wall. Rising to her feet, she paused at the sight of two little girls going through Jamanny's things. When she saw Pig and Nina, a great force pulled her back into the dark closet. Into the hall, Dozer slings her into the wall, kicking her back down the stairs.

Jamanny's leg was bleeding. Having Faith in the house didn't sit well with him. Out of all the victims he had tormented, no one had ever dared to escape—and none of them ever defied him as long as Faith had.

She was a bad omen, a sign of things to come. For once, it had appeared that the world had finally rotated in his direction. He had thought his life was blessed by the divine until then. The social workers had been the tip of the ice berg. He felt that his family was slowly turning against him. He thought about the grandchild that he had locked away and his own mortality. Stabbing the knife into the floor, he knew that it would have to be a cold day in hell before he accepted death.

More weeks of suffering flew by in Jamanny's compound. The moisture from previous rains had saturated the ground and brought a moldy smell through the cold, damp guts of the house. Oppression continued as usual under the dictatorship of Jamanny as the house became more of a sealed coffin. Tilting and creaking on a bed of debris and old life, the old house sank deeper into its foundation.

Underneath it all, in the weary room, the dark began to play tricks on Faith's eyes. Memories and voices played recordings of conversations and laughter to her ears. Between being high on Jamanny's fix and getting knocked almost senseless, Faith sometimes couldn't tell the difference between hallucinating and dreaming. It wasn't until Jamanny or his sons reared their evil heads that she knew for sure that she had returned to reality.

This time, tied tightly with an electrical cord, Faith stared endlessly into the cascade of night that hung down from the ceiling. Slowly drifting in and out of conversations about anything, she burst into laughter. A low voice from the wall caused her to turn and listen.

"Who are you?"

"I don't know anymore. Who are you?" Faith laughed while crying, believing that she had completely lost her mind.

"Who are you?" the voice asked again, breaking any doubts that Faith was imagining. It tapped and slid fingers along the surface of the wood in another room. "I'm so cold, hungry, starving. What's your name?"

"Name?" The question stumped Faith for a second. "My name … is … Faith." She numbly pressed against a table, relieved that she hadn't forgotten her name.

"Don't cry. Faith, don't you ever cry for the devil! This is his kitchen. Faith is such a pretty name." The mysterious voice became more feminine, soothing. "The devil and his monster are the only ones who remain in this house now. Gotta fight until the death of your soul, child. Don't be scared, sweet child." The movement slid to the other end of the wall. "So hungry."

"I just want my daughter, my baby Destiny." Her tears soaked into the table. "Have you seen my baby?"

"Daughter? Baby? She's dead; we all dead. Wait. So beautiful she was. She slayed the demon. I loved him, so much." Her head thudded against the wall. "I'm free now. Starving, so human. I haven't eaten for … I can't remember. All that remains is the devil and the monster. The devil and his monster, the devil and his monster remains!" The voice repeated in a vicious loop, getting louder and louder until it became a woman's voice, screaming its dreadful chant.

"Leave me alone! Leave me alone. Shut up! Be quiet!" Faith yelled, hearing a door to the woman's room open.

"Both of you shut up that damn racket!"

Jamanny's voice caught Faith off guard. The sounds of him slapping and throwing the woman around in the other room signaled Faith to prepare for her turn. "That'll fix your ass! You ain't they momma now, are you? Get her arm, boy!"

"Stop, no! Never again, never again!" The woman yelled, and the wrestling calmed. "I hate you. Never will I fear … I … I'm hungry."

"Hold your dope fiend ass on! Put her ass in that corner and come on before Doza falls in love down there! We got her anytime, plus she needs to learn a lesson. We're gonna come to an understanding this time." Jamanny stomped out the room and unlocked Faith's door. "Just give her a little bit; she don't need much." As the light from the hall filled the room, he took one look at Faith and smiled wickedly. "Ah, there's my girl, let me look at ya." He grabbed her face and stared into her pupils. "How's the chin?" He tapped her jaw with the back of his hand as she twitched in pain. "Healing just fine, good. You know, it really does smell down here. How do you do it? Did you take a crap again?" Jamanny laughed, strutted to the head of the table, and leaned over her. "Nah. That's right; you ain't had nothing to eat. Darn it, I've been forgetting to feed you!" He pinched her swollen, aching cheek. "Today, I'm all healed up from your little stab wound, but I ain't gonna touch you just yet. I'm going let your new boyfriend, little Timothy in there, have his way with you first. He's just like a baby wild bull under the sheets."

"What do you want? Wasn't Big Momma enough?" Faith uttered between her barely moving lips.

"Sorry, but I can't make out a word you're saying. You'll have to speak up."

"Where's my daughter?"

"Are you still on her?" Jamanny leaned down close to her face. "Listen, I'm gonna break you down and wear you out for years and years to come. I'm gonna hurt you, starve you, and then make sweet love to you until you beg to be mine—just like I did your sweet, old grandmother." He hit the table with both hands. "I'm gonna take everything that the outside world has given you—your pride and your dignity. You're going to see how puny and weak you really are to me, and then, just when you've really, really, had enough, I'm going to do it all over again and kill you, Faith. I think I'm going to do this for Jamondo. I'm going to set you on fire and watch you burn—just like your Big Momma." He kissed Faith on the forehead and crept away. "Go on, son. Get on in here—and get it done! She's waiting for you. Come on. I don't got all day! We got other things to attend to right now."

"Ooh, I get to go two times. Yes!" Timothy hurried past his father. Carrying a used needle and half a plastic bottle, he leaned over and kissed Faith on the neck. "I'll be back for you, pretty. You finally get a chance to know me. I'm a monster." A foul of the foulest of anal wind blew from between his jagged caked teeth.

"Boy, come on with it while I'm feelin' it." Jamanny said. "You know what? I'll meet ya down there. So hurry up and put it in her!" With one last glare, Jamanny made a sucking sound and walked away.

"Now you about to feel real good after this. We going to get real close later." He wrapped a rubber hose around her arm, tightened it, and shoved in a big needle.

Faith watched him pull out the syringe, dip it in the container of solution, and refill it. "I'm going to hurt you."

"Not after this." Timothy laughed and injected her with a full needle of his father's concoction. "Take all this. Look at you. You're already fallin' in love with me. You're gonna be so wet by the time I come back. You're going to be so out of it—I ain't even gone stop either." He tried to suck on Faith's neck as she wiggled her head about. Timothy walked back into the hallway and shut the door.

"Sheer will." He said and walked away.

"I was just a little girl back then," the voice slurred from the wall. As her breathing grew louder, her slithering closer to part of the wall next to Faith made the floor creak. "Just a little baby when he found me. Always trying to be grown I was—even left the house. I was lost and then, there he was—the Satan. The Satan." The woman on the other side knocked on the wall in the midst of Faith's dizzy spells.

"What is this he keeps putting in me? What did he give me? Ahh ... what is this?" Every time Faith closed her eyes, the room started spinning. She swayed back and forth on the table, trying to cope with the effects. "What did he put in us? My muscles are burning."

"What did he put in us?" The woman on the other side pressed against the wall, tickled by the question. "Don't worry. You'll get used to it. It makes the pain all better. At first you can't take it, then you need it just to think, just to be ... normal."

"I don't want to get used to it! What is this shit? Oh." After the intense pain, Faith began to drift into a relaxed state. "Why?"

"He wants to rule us. To control the mind and spirit. Never again, never again. He couldn't take her away from me. No! Never again. Only the devil and his monster remain. Never again shall I fear; never again shall I feel pain! Never again! You run or fight until the death of your soul, Faith. He couldn't take her away from me!"

Faith thought of the time she had gone to look for information on her ex-boyfriend Jamondo. Crossing paths with a crazed woman who was active with him and his father, Faith remembered her screaming those exact words.

"Rashida?" Faith's mind drifted into the realm of her deepest thoughts. A large red plastic ball bounced off her head playfully as she found herself laughing among a group of familiar children. Covering her eyes to block the intensity of the sun, Faith stood in the shadow of a broad figure standing under a tree. "Daddy?"

Hearing gunshots, she turned to see the face of a younger Jamanny hanging a pistol out of a moving vehicle. Returning to her father, she stood before his grave. "No, why did you have to go? Daddy!" A great sadness came over her. Sulking in regret, a downpour of rain suddenly showered her body.

On a street, someone walking past placed an umbrella over her head. Glancing at the umbrella's material and then up at the person she shared it with; there was something about those eyes and teeth. They belonged to the same one who raped her, stalked her, and pretended to be a stranger off the street—Jamondo.

She felt herself being grabbed and choked in the hall of her best friend's apartment. She opened her eyes to the sight of a newborn baby in her arms. Inside a hospital room, Nurse Julia and Nodia smiled joyously at her. Faith watched speechlessly; her friend's skin melted from their muscles as they fell to the floor in howling screams.

Inside her grandmother's burning house, Faith's mouth hung open at the sight of Jamanny standing next to some creature. His body was engulfed in flames—except for his head. He held Destiny in midair with his right hand.

"Every princess has to have faith, and in your faith, you will find your destiny. It doesn't matter what you do. Don't you pray?" Faith heard her grandmother's words clearly. Stripped of life and loved ones, her eyes stared into Jamanny's glowing, demonic eyes. Tired of life on this planet, she boiled with anger and hatred. As he smiled, demons surround her, and her hands changed into large black claws.

"Only the devil and his monster remain in the house now," Rashida blurted.

Faith joined her in a horrific scream that could be heard through every vent in the house.

"Sounds like our little guest." Timothy was gathering tools inside the underground hall. His father was checking a power box. "I think she's ready for me."

"You better hope so because that didn't sound like no friendly scream. That ain't sound quite right. Doza, lock up them parts for me!" Jamanny yelled. "Timmy, check and see what that ruckus was all about. You better not have killed that gal before I had my fun with her!" He adjusted the crotch of his overalls and wiped the sweat from his face. "You might wanna take a look upstairs too; it ain't no tellin' what them gals gettin' into."

He proudly watched Timothy follow his instructions. He had a feeling that something wasn't right. Spotting a pot of moldy tomato soup that he had fed to Junior, he kicked it in the direction of his son.

"Eh, and feed her this shit! Make sure she eats every bite too. Shit stinks!" Journeying down the corridor, Timothy was happy that he didn't have to share a rape victim with his brother or father. Taking off his ripped shirt, he caught a glimpse of blood on his hands. Wiping them on his pants, he noticed all the lights out in the hall ahead.

Only a single blinking bulb dangled from a wire in front of Faith's cell. Slowing his stride, he stepped on broken glass. He giggled at the feeling of being a little helpless. A growl sent Timothy jumping three steps ahead.

"Shut up, Junior! I know what I'm doing! You dang near gave me a heart attack. I know you hear me! Pops, why don't you put a muzzle on him sometimes?" He stormed to the door. Fixing himself up, he wiped his sweaty hands on his shirt and tossed it into the shadows of the hall. "Was that you who was calling me just a little while ago? Well, I'm here. I've been saving myself for you too. You ready?" He looked into the small window of the door at the view of torn loose wires and an empty table. Cleaning the window off, he strained to see what wasn't there.

"Where the heck did you go?" Fumbling with a ring of keys, he slid the key in the keyhole to learn that he didn't lock the door. Opening the door, he became frustrated. "It's like she's a ghost." He looked into the room in fear of what his father would do when he got the news. Putting the smelly rusty pot down, he turned to leave.

"Shit!" he whispered, just before receiving a sharp pain in his neck. As his oxygen cut off, five sharp nails dug into his Adam's apple, yanking him back into the room. By the throat, he was flipped over the table, tumbling into the wall and floor. Before he could fully recover, he was grabbed by the hair and his head was banged against the edge of the table repeatedly.

Faith beat Timothy with the large left pot of inedible goo, spilling its contents all over him and the floor. "You can't have my soul; you can't have me!" Faith put Timothy in a headlock and knocked holes in the walls with his face. Seeing nothing but demons and flames around her, she hallucinated her nails sprouting into giant eagle talons. With a sense of spiritual awakening and the spirit of GOD with her, she wrestled and shred through the entities of darkness, tearing them apart with her claws, trying to reach the devil and her daughter.

Hollering for dear life, Timothy bought some time to escape Faith's wrath. He kicked her into the shadows. Running out of the room, she scratched him deeply several times, drawing more blood. Squeezing out the door, he slammed it and ran to his father.

"What in tarnation?" Jamanny said. Faith burst through the door, pulling the last bulb down. "Aw hell naw!" He stood in total blackness as erratic screams and howls filled the hall. "Timothy?" He searched for his cigar lighter. Hearing his son plead for help, he started to worry and went for his gun. Without warning, he fell victim to the merciless attacks, joining his son in yells, yips, and prolific swearing.

The hall drew quiet and calm as Timothy found his lighter. In three clicks, he flicked a trembling flame between them. "Where did she go?" On the goop, grime and dirt covered floor, Timothy extends the light in front of him as his father pans around with his arm. "Where is she?"

"How the hell am I supposed to fuckin' know where she went? It's darker than a coon's hole down here! What I want to know is how the hell did she get out after you? Idiots!" Jamanny stared at his son's bleeding scratches on his face. Pushing himself up from the floor, he dusted himself off and pulled out his pill bottle.

"And what the hell's wrong with her? Why is she so goddamn strong? She's been tied up down here for a hundred years." Faith silently appeared next to him.

"Only Satan remains, never again!" Faith hit him with a club like object. "Never again!" She dashed off.

"She sounds like the other one, Pops! Ow!" Timothy cried as he and his father get their butts kicked at the same time.

"Turn on the light! Fix the goddamn lights!" The old man was knocked down every time he tried to figure out where to run. As the fighting progressed, they heard footsteps near them. Then, just as quickly as it started, the battle ended in a faint moan. Faith fell next to them, and Dozer stood over them all, holding a small torch and a large piece of plywood.

Jamanny turned to Timothy. The empty container of his toxic drug rolled and touched his hand. He smacked him on the head at the precise time of contact with the bottle. "Damn, son. What's that smell? How much of that shit did you give her—a whole dose?" He grabbed his sore shoulder and twisted his aching back, producing a loud pop.

"No, five." Timothy rubbed his head.

"Five! Five doses?" Jamanny's mouth fell open, and his head hung low. "Goddamn boy, goddamn." He looked down at Faith's body. "Don't give her no more of that shit for a while. No more."

Chapter 9:
THE REUNION

———— ✳ ————

The sun scraped across the Jamanny's ashy land, penetrating the poorly fortified fortress. Shining through the sides of sheets and covers that had been used as curtains in the boarded windows, bright beams shined through holes along the roof and walls of the building. Magnified by the window's glass, traveling through floating lint and dust, a single ray of solar energy landed upon the small hand of a child. Feeling the concentration of warmth, small green eyes opened, watching the heavenly spotlight. Even though this place was full of doom and misery, inside the gloom, it continuously appeared and was proven that all the darkness and evils of the house couldn't stop the natural light of GOD.

On the top floor, inside the children's closet, beneath the hanging clothes, between piles of old shoes and unworn denim, Nina awakened from a restless nightmare. On her belly, she rolled her head upright, glancing around the room. With no sight of Pig in her bed or the baby boys huddled beneath the covers, she stretched out from what remain of her palette. Wiping her face, she looked down at her scarred hand and walked out.

Inside the playroom, her attention was directed to odd noises from the hall. Placing an ear upon its surface, she turned the knob and cracked it open. Lamond and Omack galloped in, laughing and screaming, almost taking her with them. Running in a circle around her, they went back into the hall laughing. Floating to Tina's bedroom door, she scooted quietly beside Pig. "What are—"

"Shhhh!" Pig raised her index finger to her lips and grinned.

Hearing the familiar awkward compliments and unpleasant sounds of incest, Nina made a distraught face, accidently creaking open the door.

"What the heck?" Timothy, caught off guard, pressed their sister Tina's head down against the dresser, steadily pumping her from behind.

"Close the door and get out! Close the door now!" Tina yelled as the dresser bumped against the wall.

"Get before you get it!" Red in the face, Timothy held her down with one hand, held up his pants with the other, and winked.

In disgust and shock, Nina swiftly closed the door and shrugged her shoulders free of chills and sick thoughts. Used to seeing her sister in disagreement of the sausage treatment, Nina said, "Yuck! Why do they keep doing that? And I thought that she didn't like to?"

"You can't believe her; she's a liar," Pig said.

"What do you mean? She never really lied to me. Did she?" Nina stirred up scenes and episodes in the back of her mind. "You lie too! You always lie!"

"Yeah, but I am kidding; she's a liar. You have to watch her. They all lie except for me and the twins. Tina's really sneaky and evil like Daddy," Pig said in a low tone as they entered the room and shut the bedroom door. "You can't trust her; she's mad."

"What do you mean? Why is she so upset? She can't be mad; she was smiling when the door opened!"

"I think she misses our brother. She loved him a whole lot. I used to see them on top of each other all the time."

"Ew. More brothers and sisters. This family is nasty."

"I know. At first, it was just like with Timothy Daddy made them kiss, and then they started liking it and doing it all the time on their own. All the time!" Pig said.

"What happened to him? What was his name?"

"His name was Jamondo; he was way older than Dozer. Daddy told us that some woman fell in love with him. Our brother didn't like her, and she didn't want anybody to be with him, so she killed him. One night, in revenge and honor of his son, Daddy dressed Tina up in some clothes and sent her to burn the woman's house down, but I think she killed her. A true story, Miss Rashida knows it; she was there. But ever since that happened, Tina's been a real meany. When you're not around, she talks about what if he was still around … our brother."

"I've been downstairs." Nina leaned into her ear. "In the basement."

"You went back down there? Why? You could have been eaten!" Pig's voice slightly rose. "Mom's not down there—remember?"

"I know, but where is she? Tina's a liar; remember?" Nina threw her sister's words back at her. "She never told us about her! She never tells us anything about our mom like she promises. But I've been down there. I've been down there exploring, and there's a woman down there! It's been a while, but I think it's that woman who kept getting into the house. Remember that? She's still down there and she's been down there for a while!"

"Nina, leave her alone. You've seen what Daddy does to them people. Remember the piles of bones? Our mother is dead, and she's been dead a long time! She ain't ever coming back. You have to accept it." Pig, tired and frustrated by the conversation, was done with the topic for good.

"I heard talking through the vents. Someone's looking for their daughter! I think it's her!"

"Nina, you said she's looking for a daughter. There's three girls here! She's not our mother, so just leave it! Daddy probably killed her daughter just like he's gonna do to us sooner or later! You better stay out from down there before he punishes us all. I'm not ready to die in that grave we dug yet."

They heard their father's boots on the stairs.

"That's my son. Get her good, boy!" Jamanny drunkenly opened Tina's door. Shutting it, he staggered in the direction of the playroom.

"Oh no, I forgot. Nina, he's coming for me. Help me." Pig started crying. "You have to run away."

"Why? What's wrong, Pig? What did you do?" Nina watched her sister break down as their father tried the door. "Why are you crying?"

"It's my turn, Nina; it's my birthday." Pig bravely wiped away her tears as Jamanny swung open the door.

As it slammed into the wall, Jamanny leaned against the uneven doorway. "Pig?" He called in a deep watery voice, reeking of tainted, potent liquors. Already in a deep sweat, he wiped his mouth and stepped into the room. "My favorite pet, come to me. Come to your father, child. You know what day it is; don't you?" He stared into Pig's face, but she tried not to make eye contact. "Let's go." He took her by the arm and pulled Pig away. Pig walked slowly beside him, looking back. "Happy Birthday." Jamanny stopped at the door and smiled at Nina.

Slowly dropping her arms from her sister, Nina watched the madman leave. Nina screamed out for Pig, but no sound came out. Listening to them inch down the hall, she ran to the door as Omack and Lamond ran in. Peeping outside the room, Nina saw her father take her sister into Rashida's old bedroom. Hearing the ongoing unholy sex of her older siblings, she returned to the playroom, closed the door, and cried with her back against it. Looking across the room at her innocent brothers, she thought about the day when they would be forced to have sex with them also. And it struck her, how hard it was to leave that house.

Eventually falling into a tearful sleep, Nina realized that an hour had passed since she had seen Pig. Lamond and Omack were playing with two wooden cars. She slipped out from the confines of the closet. Easing open the door, she poked her head into the hall, then quietly inched her body behind it.

"Nina?" A faint voice startled her. Pig was staggering against the wall with stains of red on her gown.

Running to her sister's side, she hugged her softly. Placing one of Pig's arms over her shoulders, Nina wrapped her arm around her waist for support. "Pig, you're hurt. What did he do to you?" She moved her away from the door. "Where'd he go? Where is he?"

"He's sleeping." Pig's weak legs trembled beneath her as the handprint on her face throbbed.

Making it to the playroom, they closed the door. They heard stomping inside the hallway. Nina and Pig prayed that it wasn't their father or older brothers coming for seconds or thirds. Having just gotten away, any of their older siblings surely would send Pig back into the room with Jamanny. As the footsteps neared, their hearts dropped. Crossing their toes and fingers, they sighed in relief when Tina walked in. She had left Timothy asleep inside her room.

Shutting the door behind her, Tina looked at them with the same dilated pupils that Rashida had. She struggled to keep her balance. Tilting her head to the side, she stared at them without saying a word. She knelt between them. "While they're sleep, I need to show you something."

"Timothy! Come on, son, we have to go now. We're late!" Jamanny stepped out of Rashida's room. "Timothy?" He snapped the straps on his overalls. Timothy opened Tina's door and ran out.

"Coming, Pa." Timothy straightened his clothes, trying to wake completely up.

"Where are all my goddamn clothes? I ain't got none up here either! Let's go, boy; time to go to work. I didn't know it was this late. Tina! You got the house, gal. Take care of Junior for me, and that's it! Bring your ass right back upstairs when you're done. And Nina, feed that damn dog too!" He walked down the stairs, and Timothy following drowsily.

"All right!" Tina said. She waited by the window for them to leave. "Good, they took Dozer with them; they're all gone." She looked down at Pig's bloody garment; it reminded her of when Jamanny and her brothers had done the same thing to her when she was a little girl. "First, let's do something about this." Although somewhat high off her father's drug, she still appeared to be quite sane and functional.

With no doctor, medical attention, or adult supervision, Tina and Nina did the best they could to accommodate Pig. They checked her private area for serious injuries. They cleaned her up and soaked her in a stinging tub of warm Epsom salt. They stood under a secret hatch that only their father, Miss Rashida, Tina, and Pig knew about. Inside the bedroom, they stared at a false section of the ceiling that could be moved. With a chair, a small body could easily fit into the rectangular opening. They sat in the attic among crates of paper, trash, and clutter.

Tina said, "Rashida used to bring us here to read. That's why we know things. This is where Daddy keeps his important papers."

"I don't believe this—another secret!" Nina sat between Tina and Pig. The attic was a small place; the entire floor was at chest level. Anyone entering would immediately have to bow down. Bats and mice squeaked from the shadows, the smell of mold and old newspaper choked them. Splashes of poo in the far corners of the room also explained the odors.

"You okay, Pig?" Nina asked.

Pig pulled a tooth out from her bottom row of teeth. "Yep." She looked down at the tiny tooth in her palm and thought about when Jamanny had struck her.

"It's a mess in here! How often do you come up here?" Nina did not know what to touch or where the cleanest area to rest her hand was. "It's nasty up here."

"We come up here whenever we want to, but Daddy doesn't know!" Tina dug into a pile of paper and clothes. "Look, I found this!" She slapped a stack of newspapers between them.

"Great. I can barely read, and she can't read," Pig said. "Real smart."

"Newspapers, Tina?" Nina said. "What do these have to do with anything?"

"Look!" Tina held up a newspaper to her face. "It's Daddy. I found a crate with all kinds of stories with him in them."

Lifting the crinkled article, Nina saw Jamanny in a photo of a car wreck. "So?"

"So? In all of these articles, people have died or gotten hurt. He's in a bunch of them—him and this lady!"

"So what? We already know he kills people!" Pig said.

"Right. Why did you bring us here? We are in enough trouble as it is, Tina! I'm walking the dog; you're high!" Nina searched for the hatch.

"What? Wait! This one happened around the time you came. I know because we came here. It says a bad accident happened between two vehicles. A whole bunch of people got hurt too. A lady named Faith Hopkins survived, but her daughter was thrown from the car, and the body was never found." She sorted and folded numerous clippings and articles about the woman and her father. "This one says the woman was put in the hospital in critical condition. That means she was hurt really bad. It says she was paralyzed; her body couldn't move."

"It's the lady I saw in the basement!" Nina whispered in Pig's ear as they looked at each other with open mouths.

"I think that's why we had to move. He got in trouble for that accident," Tina said.

"What if he's running? Maybe if we get out of here, we could use this stuff to get him in trouble," Pig suggested.

"Poor Rashida, I wonder if she knew something—or was she in on it too?" Nina looked through more newspapers.

"I dunno. I just figure out things by myself. I don't read all that good, but I know some words and how to sound them out. I'm gonna read some more. I been thinkin' what if you're her daughter?" Nina and Pig glanced at each other. "Ever wonder how come you two are nearly the same age? Nina, we just met you not that long ago. You were just a baby. If she was our mom, how come she just kept you?" She held back her tears.

"If she's her mother, then where's ours?" asked Pig.

"I think Daddy killed her and our brother." Tina broke into tears.

Nina rewound their conversation in the back of her mind, darting off to the basement at full throttle. Thinking of Rashida's mix of jumbled speeches and all the possible lies that Jamanny could have told her, she raced downstairs to his room. Diving into the messy closet, she found the wooden covering and threw it to the side. She hurried down the old crumbling staircase. The heat and humidity hit her, followed soon by an unsettling coolness. Down the corridor of rats and cockroaches, she began to check the rooms, knocking on locked doors. "Momma!" She was struck by the feeling of death in every direction. Peeking through the cracks and holes in the wall, she desperately searched for the woman.

Hearing strange noises, fear overcame her. She bravely called the woman's name. "Faith Hopkins!" Nina's voice cracked as she saw movement coming from under the door in front of her. "Momma? Faith!" She twisted the knob, revealing a woman, chained to the ceiling and nailed to a board.

"Help me," she said, dripping blood. Her eyelid had been carved out.

Nina ran out of the room, slamming the door behind her. Resting against the door, she prepared herself to see bad things and hurt people in need of help. Slowing her breathing and pulse, the vibration of rattling chains went through her body. Turning around, she gathered herself and neared the door across from her. The knob did not open. Too short to see through the small window, she jumped up and down in place to see inside.

A powerful feeling of hope rose through the madness and everything bad she had experienced. The possibility that it would soon be over radiated inside her—along with the idea of living a normal life. She found a ring of keys on a nearby chair and unlocked the door. "Mommy!"

Nina froze. The naked woman chained to the floor resembled a beaten, mutilated version of the woman in the newspaper. "Faith Hopkins?" She slowly walked up to the woman, sickened by the foam that ran from her mouth.

Faith's mouth trembled as though she was talking, but from another place. Without a sound, she trembled and shook.

"Faith, I know who you are. I know what happened to you. What happened to your baby?" Nina looked down at her arm and legs, noticing many needle tracks and scars. "He shot you with drugs; didn't he? Faith?" Nina stepped around the old mattress that Faith sat on. Pressing on Faith's arm, Nina gently tapped her forehead as Faith came too.

Wobbling in place, Faith nodded in and out, trying to make sense of the spinning room.

"Faith, wake up! Faith, snap out of it. Fight it! Where do you think your daughter is? What happened to her? Faith?" Nina heard someone coming. Not caring anymore about the rules of Jamanny, she shook the heavily sedated woman and said, "Faith, what happened to her? Do I look familiar? Look at me. Get up! Faith, what's your daughter's name? Get up!" The footsteps grew closer. "Look at me! Who am I? Momma?" Faith fell over as Nina cried hopelessly over her. "Momma. Faith. I need to know something." Her tears trickled as the footsteps ended, Tina stood in the doorway quietly. "Faith?"

"She's gone; isn't she? Come on, Nina." Pig hobbled over to Nina, pulled her up, and slowly walked back to the door.

"Destiny, I love you," Faith mumbled, touching Nina's soul as she turned and ran to her.

"Mommy, I'm sorry!" Destiny cried. "I'm sorry, Momma."

"Destiny, it's you. You found me." Not knowing if she was still dreaming, Faith indulged in the moment. Wearily she raised the heavy chains and hugged what looked like an older version of her baby. "Never again."

She passed out as Tina braced against the frame of the door. Nina sat on the floor, rocking the body of her abused mother under the dim light of the flickering candle.

Chapter 10:
FAITH'S REVENGE

———— ✳ ————

Right under Jamanny's nose, a great movement began to conspire directly inside the heart of the house. After years of abuse and violence, a mini revolt manifested within the hearts and minds of his children. A premeditated escape plan transpired between Destiny and Pig—with its flaws and uncertainties. Since they couldn't just up and leave the house anytime they wanted, they soon realized that they had to wait for the right opportunity. Knowing that there was no guarantee that her mother would live to see the next day, Destiny's love and anxiety to see her mother free convinced her to act immediately. Executing a move at night was her best bet but would still be an obstacle.

Jamanny and his sons had been lurking beneath the house for hours. Faith was forced to listen to the unspeakable acts upon Rashida in the room next to her. As if doubling and tripling up on her wasn't enough, Faith got a glimpse of the monstrous shadow cast by Junior as they walked him to Rashida's room. Passing Faith's door, the sound of his feet indicated his size. Through a small crack in the wall, Faith saw what awaited her.

Breathless at the thought of having a single encounter with the massive man, she was captivated by the giant's savage mating behavior. Only able to see Rashida's legs and lower torso, the large form swallowed Rashida's small, battered frame. As Timothy held her hands, stretching her arms from one end of Faith's old table, Junior hunched over her from behind like a horse in heat. Jamanny stood off to the side, pressing down on her back with one hand, squirting a tiny bottle of lubricant between her and his son. Faith felt her pain, witnessing helplessly the old man forcing his innocent children to perform inhumane acts.

"Get it, Junior. It's good; ain't it? It's nice and soft, remember? Harder—just like I taught ya now!" Junior's deformed face stared blankly into the abyss. "Did you fasten that gal's door back, boy?" He looked at Timothy with beady eyes.

"Yep, I did. I swear I did, Pops!" Timothy said, smiling.

"Doza! Go check that goddamn door!"

Dozer was standing silently nearby. Hearing him run off down the corridor, he glanced back at Timothy like a hungry pit bull.

"Son, let me explain this to you for the thousandth time! How do we suppose to keep them in if you keep letting them out? Use your brain sometimes, boy!" Jamanny smacked Timothy on the head.

Stuffed into a open robe with the sleeves torn off, a stained and dingy plain T-shirt the size of a gown, expanded around two large breasts and an extremely wide, bulging belly. Junior's large forearm guided a plump hand, twice the size of his father's, up and down on what Faith could only describe as a long bending, baby elephant penis. Adding to the malevolence, Jamanny grabbed the extending pulsating erectile muscle and thrashed it into Rashida as the two let loose an incredible harmony of screams. Frantically rocking, without warning, Junior shoved Jamanny back into the opposite wall and hollered a lengthy thunderous roar of gibberish.

Feeling between Rashida's legs, the feeble monster smelled his fingers and licked them. Releasing a dark grunt of a laugh, Junior reached for his brother, pushing deep into Rashida's vagina. Pushing forward wildly, he snapped free of her and went after Timothy. Pinning his brother between the wall and the table, he locked onto his back, attempting to thrash him with hard swift stokes of manhood.

As the boy squeezed away from the table, his father took control of his large son and walked him back over to Rashida. As they slowly moved, Faith caught the sight of thick white drool that hung and dripped from Junior's mouth. Turning her head, Rashida screamed in excruciating pain. Her cry rose over the sudden pounding of flesh against the squishy, watery smacking noise. Floored by the suffering, Faith lowered her head in pain and anger, beginning to scream in protest. "That's enough. Leave her alone! She's the only one who's been there for you, you maggot! Leave her alone!" Her voice rattled the wires that held her mouth closed.

"Oh you just don't quit; shut up! Don't you worry your pretty little head because you're next!" Jamanny walked out the room. "Keep your eye on them, Timmy. This one's talkin' again!"

He entered Faith's cell; Faith was securely chained and bolted to the floor. "First I'm gonna do your little sweet ass personally, and then today, I'm gonna let these three boys teach you a little something about manners. And don't worry, Junior's gonna love you." He unbuttoned his shirt and smiled.

"Dad, we got an emergency! He killed her. Timothy killed her!" Dozer rushed his brother inside the room, and they began scuffling as the tussle moved into the open hall. "Son of a bitch! Why'd you do it? You knew she was mine!" Dozer's choked his brother as Jamanny broke them up. "We could go to prison for this, dumbass! I hate you!" He threw punches as Timothy blocked and ducked into a bear-hug, taking more body blows.

"Calm down, boy. Get a hold of yourself right now!" Jamanny extended both arms between them. "Now wait a cotton-pickin' minute! What the fuck's going on? What just happened? Did I miss something?"

"He killed her, Dad. He tore her insides out! It's a mess; blood's all over the place!"

"What?" Jamanny's puzzled face melted into an angry frown as he looked at Timothy.

"Ha! I don't know what he's talkin' about, Pops! I ain't done nothing! Ha!"

"Son, if it's true what he says you did ... don't get your panties in a bunch, Doza. Both of you, take your brother back to his room and lock it up. Then bring your behinds back here, and meet me near the storage."

"Where's my friend, you asshole?" Faith looked at Jamanny as he slammed the door. "Where's Julia? And where's my daughter? Where are they?" She listened to them move around, thinking that Julia might be dead. The boys wrestled Junior out the room,

"Rashida? They didn't shut the door! Get out of there! Rashida?" Faith stretched the chains over to the wall. Trying to make a bigger hole in the crack that she could all ready see through, the two-inch hole that easily crumbled into a six-inch entrance. "Rashida, are you still there? Rashida? Oh no." Faith could see a burnt leg propped against the bottom of the table leg, not moving. "Rashida." She sat back in the quietness of the flickering darkness.

"They hurt me bad, Faith," Rashida's said. "He got me again. I barely can move."

"Don't speak if you don't have too! Rashida, rest!" They both had gained a great compassion for one another. "If I get out of here, I'm taking you with me. I swear! I would battle it out right here!"

Rashida laughed painfully. "Such a heart ... for a place like this, must ... be ... of GOD. Talkin' helps. Once I was blind, but you came and saved me, allowed me to see a little better. Even though he did all those terrible things to you, you still give him shit." Breathing loudly, Rashida choked out another snorting laugh. "You've been more help to me than you'll ever realize. Out of all this, you never blamed me. You are truly special. I think this is the first time we're both sober." She made them both laugh. "Faith, I am truly sorry for everything."

"I forgive you. You were with the devil." Faith put her hands in the praying position.

Further down the corridor, inside what looked like a storage area, Jamanny and his sons opened the door to a scene of a bloody massacre. The torture area had been transformed into a slaughterhouse of Tausha's blood and mangled organs. On a conveyor belt, her intestines had been pulled and stretched all around the room.

Trying to estimate the cleanup job, Jamanny lifted the front of his boot and tapped it on the floor. "This is one hell of a job, son—another one. This is gonna stink like hell." There was so much blood that it was impossible for them to avoid stepping in it. Jamanny twisted his lips around a broom straw and flicked the bill of his hat. "Now Timothy, she sure ain't good to us dead, now is she?" Proud of the boy's murderous tendencies, but more angered by his constant disobedience, the father thought of a suitable punishment. "I'll take care of the girl for now. Doza, why don't you take your brother and go play with Junior for a while? Don't leave him; he's gonna need help gettin' him off. Just make sure he learns what it means to follow instructions and not to lie." He winked at Dozer and turned his back to them.

"Take me to what? Pops? No!" Timothy laughed and kicked as Dozer manhandled him out the room.

Jamanny found a barrel and duffle bag for the corpse. He tossed her in a cart and followed the boys to Junior's nest. Timothy cried in pain as Dozer held his arms. Junior took an held around his waist, ramming him from behind. "Not too long, boy. Remember he's still your brother."

"Get him off me, Pa! Swear I'm sorry for lying and everything! Get him off me! Give me a chance, please! Get him the fuck off me!" Timothy hollered and squirmed as Junior lifted him up and pinned him over the back of his chair.

"Let this be a good lesson to you, son. When you go against me, you get fucked. Doza, you heard what I said—not too long now. You kiddies play nice." He returned to the body in the hall. While he tended to the disposal, Dozer peeped into the hall to make sure he was gone. He shut the door and walked away from the room.

"Faith?" Sharp pains flowed through Rashida's body. "I have to tell you something; I don't think I got too long."

"Yes, Rashida."

"Wait. Someone's coming." Rashida said as Dozer crept past their rooms. Returning to silence, a light mist settled inside the shadows.

"Rashida? Rashida?" Faith received no response. As she began to think bad thoughts, two coughs jumpstarted her heart.

"Faith, when he took your child, I knew you'd come. I wanted to help. Your child helped me too."

"Rashida, it's okay. I forgive you!" Faith searched the room for anything to pick the locks on the chains.

"Listen. I helped him build this shithole of a house, piece by piece. I knew, one day, I might have to fight my way out. So I put things in the walls, Faith—gifts for you to use against him." Rashida's voice faded out.

"Rashida? Rashida, what? Rashida!"

Someone running in her direction sent her jumping back. Not seeing anyone in the window at the top of the door, she could plainly see the shadow of two feet at the bottom. Listening, she braced herself for another attack as someone jiggled the handle and unlocked the door.

The door slowly squeaked open. Like a holy cherub drawn down in the darkest of hours, Destiny stood inside the doorway. "I came to save you, Mommy. I have keys!"

Like the most beautiful dream, Faith breathed a pleasant breath at her child's expression. Her arms extended out to Destiny's first step. A dark hand reached from behind her and grabbed the back of her neck. In front of a tall dark silhouette, Faith's chance for freedom was pushed away and Destiny was yanked off her feet.

Keys fell to the dirt floor in a light cloud of smoke between Jamanny's legs. "Really? Really? Did you really think this was going to happen?" He dangled the little girl in front of her mother and threw her to the floor between them. "Congratulations, Nina. You found your bitch of a mother! I tried to warn you. I tried to keep you away from it all. Now you're gonna die with her!" He dragged Destiny out of the room, furiously slamming the door. He took her upstairs.

"Burn in hell! Let go of her! Give me my little girl!" Faith screamed and yelled as tears fell uncontrollably. "Destiny. Destiny!" She hit the floor and knocked a pan against the wall. Spilling its liquid contents all over the floor, it rattled in a spinning motion in front of her. Crying, her head touched the floor. The drops of spilled liquid dripped through the cracks of the floor, catching her attention.

"Don't cry, child. The LORD doesn't bring us this far for nothing. Remember the walls, Faith. You can move through the house behind them without … without being seen. You have to … move quickly … if you make it. My time's about up."

Faith looked down at the dark wooden floor. "It's over for me, Faith. If you ever make it out of this place, kill the devil and save my kids. The walls …" Rashida broke into what may have been her last cry as Faith touched the cracked, crumbling, and deteriorating floor beneath her. "They can't ever get enough of hurting you. Never again shall I fear; never again shall I feel pain."

In the hellish pit of a room, Rashida's words suddenly became a tool of empowerment. Faith thought about all the pain inflicted by Jamanny and his sons—and all the days she bled and fought to hold on, nearly freezing inside the icebox. All the times she was hosed down in that room, hundreds of urinations, and plenty of times when she kicked, knocked, or spilled liquids across that black floor—inside that same room she thought of as a godless room. All the days of Faith's suffering finally coming to her aid. Getting an idea, she twirled the chain around her arms, wrapping them around her hands tightly. Pulling the chains with all her strength; due to the spills and clumsy torture tactics, underneath her tired, sore and deeply bruised feet, a superb melody of rotting wood, cracked and split the warped floor.

"You have to run or fight until the death of your soul. Only Satan … and … the monster remain." Rashida's last words repeated in the back of Faith's mind.

Pulling upon the chains with every ounce of strength in her body, Faith tried to stand at the same time. "Never again." The floor popped and broke as Faith attempted to uproot the bolted portion of the chains from the floor. In snapping wood and shooting dust, the chains took flight in all directions.

In a triumphant boost of energy and loud grunts, Faith freed herself from the custody of the floor. Falling back, close to the wall, Faith slowly stood like a champion boxer over a knocked-out opponent. Life lost and dreams shattered, again she rose to the occasion of living as the power and reality of existence of the one and true GOD, manifested and shined upon her.

"We're getting outta here, Rashida. Hold on." She looked down at the chains that were wrapped around her waist and ankles with locks. Faith's words became meaningless again. "Keys?" In her mind, she pictured her daughter dropping a set of keys by the door. Squatting low enough to see under the door, the keys were covered in a bed of dirt.

Hurrying, Faith tried the knob several times with no success. The door began to rattle and shake as her fingers could be seen from the outside, stretching under the door, trying to reach the keys. "Damn it!" She stayed flat on her stomach with her feet and torso still chained to the floor. Thinking of nothing but her child and the danger she was in, Faith's skimmed the room again and looked at the holed, collapsing, boarded walls that imprisoned her. Glancing at the chains, she came up with one last attempt. Firm and steady, she pushed the chain in a straight line under the door. Carefully fishing for the set of keys, she soon pulled them under the door with the chain.

Picking up the ring of keys, she unlocked all the chains. Grabbing one, she wrapped it around her right hand and forearm. "The walls." Faith remembered Rashida's words. "I'm going to kill this cheap son of a bitch!"

She punches a hole through the wall beside the door and unlocked it. Opening the cell to Rashida, Faith walked over to her. Severely burnt, broken, and way more abused than she was, Rashida shivered and fought to breathe on the cold floor in front of her.

"Rashida, I'm Faith. I'm going to get you out of here, but I have to find my daughter before he kills her." Leaving her, she paused at the door. "Julia ..." She remembered her friend, and Jamanny's two goons, his sons whom still roamed around.

Hoping that her friend was still alive and just as well preserved as she was, Faith turned back into the room. Thinking of how her friend had given up everything out of love to help her, she glanced down at Rashida and back at the wall behind her. Her life, all the way up to this point, flashed through her mind. Thinking of how to take them all on, she began breaking through the bottom of the wall, popping and snapping wilted wood until she had created a small entrance that she could crawl through.

In a narrow space that ran and climbed through most portions of the lower structure of the house, under the light from one of the cells that penetrated through the wall, Faith could make out a butcher knife stabbed inside of one of the wooden frames. Behind her, slightly further down, she also could make out a pair of garden shears in the corner of the passage. Smiling at all the signs of a troubled and scorned woman, she went for the knife and continued down the hall, peeking through walls in search of her friend.

The path behind the drywall and wood was as limber and unsteady as the house was. Faith had no time to think of a full plan, but she knew that she had to move quickly and strike hard in order to save her daughter. In her heart, GOD was with her and had a greater plan for her. Pushing on, glancing down at her feet, Faith noticed that in some areas, she was able to see clearly down into deeper unknown levels of the building. Faith had no time for clumsy mistakes; this was it—her last opportunity to escape.

"Where the hell did she go? Fuckin' kids bit a chunk right outta my hand!"

Jamanny stormed down the stairs after making sure that all the other children were in their rooms and out of the way for the handling of Destiny and the transportation of Tausha's body. After seeing that Pig wasn't accounted for, his blood thickened. He looked over at the window at Tina; she just sat there, perhaps high off his drugs, shaking her head, crying.

"What the hell? You high too?" He walked over to her, stooped down and grabbed her chin. "Where is she? Where is Pig? Where is she, goddamn it!" he yelled at the top of his lungs.

Suddenly hearing an odd sound, he stared through the walkway of the kitchen into the living room. Stomping toward the sound, he found Dozer rolling about on the floor, holding his head.

"Boy didn't I tell you to stay with your brother? Where is he? And what the hell are you doing?"

Looking closely, he watched Dozer trying to pull a needle out of his leg and another one out of the back of his neck. Looking for more signs of the fleeing children, Jamanny stepped back into the dining room. "What the fuck?"

He looked out the window, spotting Destiny running across the yard. Jamanny went for his rifle and ran out after her. Hopping in his van, he realized that he didn't have his keys.

"Shoot! Ain't nowhere to hide out here! Welcome to my world, Nina!" He leaped out of the van and headed in the direction where he had last seen her. "What in the world?"

He came across a trail of his missing clothes, all scattered about and torn. "What the hell she's been doing, feeding them to the dog? Nina!" He followed his clothes to the old shed out in the field in back of the house. Glimpsing the shed, he heard movement coming from the inside, which brought a smile of victory to his face. "Come here, Nina. Come and give Daddy a hug." He moved in closer. Tall grass blocked his entire view of the shed, but the top of a little girl's head could be seen in the rifle's site. "Stop hiding!"

"I'm not trying to hide!" She shoved over the two-by-four that blocked the shed doors.

"Got her." Jamanny grinned evilly. Seeing the shed doors come open, he rushed to it, coming across more of his clothing. Grinding his teeth at the sight of his underwear scattered over a clutter of bushes, he came into a clearing near the shed. Lowering his gun, he stared at a pair of familiar eyes that that didn't belong to the little girl. "Just what I need, wild possums." He thought as an inch of thick fur stood over the grass. "Wait, that ain't no possum. Mr. Tiny?"

In a low growl, Mr. Tiny sniffed the air while holding something in his mouth. Slowly spinning and rolling around in place, covered in a thick white foam of slobber, the rabies-infected hound dropped the mangled body of Tiger.

"Tiger?"

Having previously been trained everyday by Destiny to attack Jamanny's clothes, the dog's eyes met his master's eyes as the smell of Jamanny sent the deranged animal in a vicious attacking frenzy.

"Tiny! Down, boy, down! No, Tiny. Heel!" Jamanny fired his gun, missing the snapping and biting dog as two rows of large teeth clamped down on his leg. Falling into the grass, the old man squealed into the bushes, seeing Destiny running back toward the house. "I'm a get cha, you little bitch!" He knocked the dog off his leg with the gun. Taking aim, he tried to stand as the dog disappeared and leaped from the side in a counterattack. Fighting the beast off, shots followed as Destiny reentered the house on a direct path to rescue her mother.

The passageway in the walls, paved during the construction of the house, raised and lowered unevenly below the first floor. Following its sharp turns and bends, Faith squeezed between small and narrow spaces undetected. Four empty cells and portions of the wall created with poor materials suddenly were replaced by sheets of aluminum, tin, and brick.

"The red room," she said.

She peeked between the opening at pipes and brick. Inside a room of blood machines, tools, and gadgets, Faith was relieved by the sight of wet, curling blonde hair. Hurrying to the adjoining room, she followed the sound of whimpering. In front of her, a rattling water pipe knocked and dripped down on a large knot of duct tape. Some bricks were missing, and others had been replaced with outside stones. Others had fallen and collected in a pile inside the wall around the pipe.

Following the duct tape, Faith could see it extending through the wall, wrapping tightly around a pair of bruised wrists and red palms. "Julia?" she whispered, starting to free bricks from the hole. Looking down, Faith made out two long, taped legs sitting above a hanging blonde head of wild, curly hair. "Julia, its Faith! Is that you?"

"Faith?" The head of a ragged blonde lifted up and moved to her voice.

"I'm going to get you out of here. Can you walk?"

"They messed me up pretty bad, Faith. Out of all those stories that your grandma told us, now look at me. I … I'm just like her."

"I know, Julia. Don't cry. We're about to get out of this evil place. I still need your help, Julia. I found her, but now he has Destiny."

"Destiny." The reason for Julia being there in the first place rolled from her tongue. Every day, she wondered if coming had been a mistake. Every day she wondered what sort of torment her friend and child was going through, unsure if they were even living.

"I'm coming in there with you. Hold still while I cut you loose." Having acquired a small scythe used to cut down tall blades of grass, Faith sliced through the electrical tape.

"Thank God. I don't believe this! I've watched people die; I thought you were one of them. I thought he killed you." Julia shook her head in unbelievable joy. To free her legs, Faith passed her the tool through the opening.

"I know. I thought the same, but we're all still here for the time being—all three of us." Faith tried to find the easiest way to get inside to her friend. "Jay, I know you're hurt and tired, but I really need you on this one. We're going to have to work together and kick some ass to get out of here. You up for it?"

"After what they did to me—to us? Out of all those talks about her?" Julia looked down at her scarred limbs. "Your Big Momma was amazing."

"It's revenge time." Faith pushed through the corner flap of an aluminum panel.

"Shit. Someone's coming, Faith!" With hair covering most of her face, Julia lifted her head toward the shuffling coming from down the hall.

"Remember I'm right here with you! Get ready."

"What? Already? What about you? Hide or something!"

"I am. Shhh! Get ready, Jay."

Stumbling in the hall, hunched over, Timothy held his backside while giving the world a piece of his mind. "I'll teach them good about messin' with me! I'm a kill every last one of them."

He was crying and laughing at the same time. Not learning from his cruel and unusual punishment, he also had chosen the path of revenge against his brother and father by deciding to cleanse the building of all living torture victims. Checking every room for life, he stumbled into the Red Room. "Ooh wee, I almost forgot you were in here. You're about as pretty as that yellow bone we brought ya in with. Been waiting? Haven't cha? Remember me?"

He looked across the room. Julia was looking helpless and broken against the wall on the floor. Head back, she sat with both legs bent and arms positioned behind her. "Yep, they gonna pay for what they done to me. You and that other one—should make us about even. Because when you go against me, you get fucked."

He stepped in front of Julia, unfastening his pants. "Today, you're going to see why they really call me a monster. It ain't gonna be like the last hundred times."

He closed his eyes and reached for her head in hopes of forcing her into oral sex. His pants opened and tumbled as half his shirt was sliced to the floor. Stunned, he peered at Julia, standing and pointing a gardener's tool directly at him. "How the heck did you get loose?"

Faith rose out the shadows behind her friend. "You on Daddy's stuff again, ain't ya?" Timothy turned to run as Faith swung the chain from her arm, catching him around the neck.

"You're not going anywhere." Faith yanked on the chain with both hands, stopping Timothy's circulation. As the boy's throat closed, he jerked and thrashed about like a fish on a hook. "Jay, we have to kill him. Knock him out or something. He's going to warn the others!"

"All those times, you, your brothers, and that old thing of a man took advantage of me, all those times that you crawled your little half-inch ding-a-ling on top of me and had your way." Back and forth, inside her quaking and sweating hands, Julia felt the warm wooden handle of the scythe at her fingertips. Holding up the tool, she eyed the sharp, dirty blade. "Look at my face! You did this to me, you are a monster."

Julia swung underhandedly at an angle and returned with a fury of swings as Timothy did his best to dodge each random slash from the blade.

"Daddy?" Reaching for the door, Timothy's air was completely cut off.

Faith held him back with one foot braced upon a metal pole that protruded from the floor. He spun free of the chain's choking grip. Finding a twisting metal rod, he charged at both of them in retaliation. Batting the rod, using all his powers to split Faith's head in two, Julia swung, blocking his blows with the gardening tool. The metal from the blade and iron collided in sparks. Timothy folded over to the side from taking a hit from Faith's chain. Catching the chain under his left arm, he yanked Faith toward him. Kicking her in the stomach, Faith slammed against the floor. Timothy let go of the chain. He went after Julia full throttle. Also ducking and dodging for her life, Julia timed her swing, catching a few blows to the face and over the shoulders. As Timothy cocked his arm far back to break her bones, Faith stabbed him in the right leg with the long pair of scissors.

Screaming in tremendous pain, Faith's chain whipped fractures into both of Timothy's hands, forcing him to drop his weapon. Glancing down at the scissors that stuck in one side of his leg and extended out the other, he tried to stop the bleeding by applying pressure with his trembling, broken, and cracked hands. Occasionally laughing, tears ran uncontrollably down his face as he tried to hold in his yell against the pain.

"Get his legs!" Faith pointed to a fat roll of dusty electrical tape next to Julia. At the moment Jamanny's son went wild, Faith dove into Timothy's face with punches. Julia grabbed, snatched, and dragged him by the ankles. A powerful blow upside the head stunned Faith. She fell back as Julia's left hook knocked Timothy flat. Snatching a pair of bloody pliers off a stand, Faith jumped down on his chest and clutched his nose between the tool's pincers.

"Where's your goddamn Daddy? Where is he?" Faith pulled Timothy closer, twisting his nose until the skin began to tear.

"Ah! fuck you—" His sentence is interrupted by his own scream. Faith lifted him up to a seated position by his nose.

"It's lucky you're a kid; I should kill your ass." Julia secured his upper body with tape. "Give me your fuckin' hands!" She roughly bent his arms behind his back and taped his legs together. Covering his mouth, Julia stomped the scissors deeper into his bleeding leg. "Some monster."

Thinking of how they both believed that they probably wouldn't see each other again, Faith and Julia hugged thankfully. Tired and beaten, Julia gazed at Faith's wired mouth and busted, dirty face. She was weary and battered. Faith looked back into Julia's scarred, swollen, bruised face, noticing that it was missing an eye.

"You're still beautiful." Faith tore a section of Timothy's jeans and wrapped it around Julia's head, covering the empty socket.

"Lying ass." Somehow keeping a sense of humor, Julia cracked a smile and hugged Faith one more time. "Well, what now?"

"Jamanny took Destiny upstairs; he's probably trying to hurt her. She tried to save me. I have to get her." Faith rewrapped the chain around her arm and headed for the door.

"I'm taking this pole." Julia picked up Timothy's rod and poked his moaning, wiggling body. Following her friend, she left him behind, soaking into the floor.

"That older brother's out there somewhere." Faith entered the hall cautiously. Scanning to the left, down the corridor, a loud bang from the right startled her and sent Julia hurrying out with the rod drawn. Tightening her fist, Faith's stomach dropped and became weak at the sight of Destiny sneaking around the corner looking for her. "What? Destiny? Destiny!"

Once more, like a familiar dream, Faith held out her arms to embrace her daughter. And just like that, Julia witnessed the dreariness of Jamanny's black dungeon vanish for a moment. GOD was shining light inside the darkest pits of hell. Destiny ran into her mother's arms, squeezing her sore, cut body. Overwhelmed with happiness and praise, Faith fell over her daughter in tears and unconditional love. Placing her hands and the cold chains gently upon Destiny's face, Faith puckered her dry lips and gently kissed her on the forehead. "I love you, Destiny."

"I love you too, Mom. I wanna go home." Destiny looked up at her mother's black eyes.

"Where is he, baby? Where's Jamanny?"

"Outside. I left him and got away. He's somewhere looking for me." Destiny peered over at Julia—she looked awfully familiar.

"Destiny, Julia. Julia, Destiny. She was the nurse who helped bring you into the world." Faith stroked Destiny's thick hair, starting to walk and look for the way out. "You two used to be really close."

"Hello, Destiny." Julia walked next to them, carrying a metal rod and a gardening tool.

"Hi." Destiny said, walking next to her mother.

"Destiny, do you know of another way out?" Faith asked.

"No. Upstairs is the only way. I don't want to go back up there." Destiny held her mother tight. A memorable, unfortunate, unforeseen sound sent her trembling beneath Faith's arm.

"You hear that? No, wait. Stop walking." Julia stopped, paused, and listened. "I hear footsteps."

"Destiny? What's wrong?" Faith looked down at Destiny's pale face.

"Oh my gosh, what is that? Is that a person?" Julia saw and heard a pair of large dragging feet under a humongous mass down the hall—along with the slapping of wet meat. When the large man spotted them, he moved faster toward them.

"Shit. It's Junior, Jamanny's son! That boy must've left his door unlocked! Get back, Destiny!" Faith moved feet in front of her as Julia followed.

"What is that thing in his hand? A shotgun?" Julia prepared for the oversized man. "Tell me he's not doing what I think he's doing?"

"That's what he's doing." Faith unrolled her chain and drew the butcher knife.

"That's his? It's ginormous! He's going to kill us with that thing!" Julia said as the growls and snorts got louder and louder. "Don't look at it, Destiny. Turn your head!"

Huffing and puffing snot and slobber, Junior's horribly disfigured face came into view. A huge belly sat upon a set of sagging legs. In front of it all, a hairy hand stroked a long penis that extended from his hand like a king cobra. Sniffing the air, he became more aroused by their scents. Licking his drooling mouth, a deep burst of bass, sounding like it could be laughter, sent chills down their spines. Rubbing his throbbing busted head that Timothy had given him, Junior palmed his family jewels with the other hand and peered at their weapons. As if remembering a cruel strike upon his flesh or some sort of past abuse inflicted by his father, a sense of fear and danger enraged him. Screaming, he lashed out at the two women. Reaching into the darkness and grabbing a chair, he hurtled it at Faith, just missing her.

"Careful. I think he's a mental patient! Stop, Junior. Don't do it. Go back!" Screaming at Julia, veins popped out of Faith's neck. She watched Junior getting a good look at Destiny. As he went for her daughter, Faith moved between them to protect her child.

Being whipped with the chain, Junior's skin ripped with every blow, causing him to jump around in pain. He was becoming more irritated and wilder. With loud groans and shrieks, he slapped his cut arms and banged his head against the hall. Furiously punching a hole in the wall to get Destiny, Faith attacked him with the chain and knife. He knocked her body halfway into the adjoining room. Like a predator going for easy prey, Junior dashed like a crazed ox after Destiny. The sweet smell and mere murmur of the untainted child increased his hormonal thirst for penetration. He thrashed about like a beast after a mate.

"Hell no—enough of this shit." Julia leaped, swinging the scythe with all her might. Guiding the tool past the arm, she ended in a chopping motion of squirting blood.

Slapping against the dirty floor and rolling like roll of sausage, Junior's third leg landed as his nut sack spilled underneath a folding body. Screeching wails filled the air as Junior curled in the fetal position, kicking frantically. Then, catching them off guard, he sprawled out, savagely crawling for the small child.

Destiny's life flashed before her; Junior died a sudden death as her mother appeared, falling from the heavens of the darkness on top of him, burying the gardening shears deep in his back.

Rolling off of him, Faith eased to her feet and wiped the blood from her mouth. Going to her daughter, she looked back at the mentally challenged brother of the father of her child. Feeling a little remorse toward the fact that Junior's was just another innocent instrument in Jamanny's twisted world, Faith shook her head, holding her stomach.

"What a pity." Julia uncontrollably stared at the outrageous shriveling penis that shrunk inside an enlarging pool of blood. "Wow." She spit beside it and followed her companions to freedom.

Nearly taking the door off its new hinges, Jamanny stormed through the back door of the house. Breathing heavily through his flaring nostrils, his eyebrows drifted together over his eyes, almost forming the head of an arrow. Riddled in scars and holes, the missing leg of his overalls revealed several severe dog bites and missing flesh. Smearing his own blood across the floor, he dragged the limp leg behind him and listened by the hall to upstairs. Hearing small feet approaching, Jamanny aimed the rifle nervously in his shaking hands.

Lamond and Omack come into view. Lowering his gun, he grinned at them skipping by, stopping the oldest of the two. "Where's your sisters, boy?" He grabbed Lamond's chin, staring into his light green eyes.

"Tina is upstairs, and Nina is downstairs, Daddy."

"That's a good boy. You two run along upstairs or outside. Daddy's gonna clean the house."

Jamanny reloaded his gun. Then setting it down, he took the usual double dose of steroids, and took a shot of his own drug in the leg. "And Tina, I know you helping them. I'm gonna fix you too!" he yelled, remembering her unusual behavior.

Tina was hidden in the attic, listening.

Determined to cleanse his house of its current infestation, he dropped the last of his rifle ammo into his pocket and headed to the basement. "Get your ass together and help me find these gals!"

Dozer was crawling on the floor in the hall. Flipping him over, he sat him up against the wall. "Doza? Doza? Dang boy, you barely got any in ya? Seen any of your sisters?"

"I know. I know, Daddy! No, I'm almost there. I ain't never been high before." Dozer tried to stand, but the movement of the room sat him back down. "What the heck do you put in that stuff? Did you hear that noise?" He followed a sound inside the walls that only he could hear.

Jamanny shoved his son back to the floor. "Good for nothings!" He kicked open all the doors in the hall. Marching into his room, a trail of blood followed him. Facing the closet, he eased it open, pointing the barrel of the rifle into the blackness. He inched into the empty, cold feeling of nothingness. Once more forced to come to terms with reality, the world he created began to spin out of his control. Feeling the sudden familiar sensation of hollowness around him, followed by a deep chill, the bad omen he had predicted whispered in the air that it had come to pass. Refusing death at the hands of another human, his fears were replaced by adrenaline and hatred toward the world. The faint taste of demise left a bad aftertaste in his mouth. The thought of his end drawing near just couldn't be swallowed. Unwilling to submit to anything not in his favor, Jamanny pushed on into the dark space. Lamond and Omack watched him from behind.

"She's not okay. We're not going to be able to move her like this." Julia squatted, examining Rashida back below the house. "If we move her, we could injure her more. She needs an ambulance, Faith."

"Take your child. Leave me," Rashida whispered. She was suffering from broken ribs, broken legs, and other broken bones. From her back, she made peace with GOD.

"Rashida!" Faith said. "I'm going to get you out of here." She stood, peering determinedly at her daughter. Destiny was playing by the door. "How we looking, Destiny?"

"All clear." Destiny said. She was scared, but hopeful at the same time.

"Okay, this is it." Next to Rashida, Faith took a deep breath. "We're going up, Rashida. Are there any guns hidden down here?"

"No—but there is a saw." Rashida passed out at their feet.

"She's out." Julia looked down at Rashida's closed eyes and exhausted face.

"A saw?" Faith looked around.

"Some good that'll do us. We can't saw him to death." Julia held her weapon in attack mode.

"Come on, baby. Let's go. We are going to have to kill this bastard." Faith glanced at Julia.

Jamanny's underground lair taunted the child and two women with its abnormal quietness. In the midst of the occasional knocking pipes and buzzing light fixtures, unsettling tones from the far end of the hall kept them on guard.

"We're almost outta here." Destiny looked up at her mother and smiled. Between her brave mother and her faithful friend, Destiny felt a little better about confronting what awaited them upstairs.

Having almost made it out from below the house, Faith had a premonition that something terrible was about to happen. At the bottom of the staircase, she saw the old farmer lurching in the middle of the hall. On a disgruntled face, Jamanny's red eyes met hers.

"He found us. Destiny, this way!" Faith swung around, took Destiny by the hand, and ran in the opposite direction. Julia followed closely. Heading for the closest room, Faith and Julia rammed down a door with their shoulders. Jamanny fired shots in their direction, exploding portions of the wall and doorway around them. They dove to the floor, taking cover with no way out.

"Don't run. I see ya now!" Jamanny laughed as the end to his worries became clear. Reloading, his mouth watered at the chase. Popping his neck, he went after them, automatically firing upon entering the room. When the smoke cleared, he frowned at the sight of a large hole in the far wall above the floor. "Looks like I got myself a mole problem. See—what you gals don't realize is that you are my legacy! We need each other—you just don't know it. See, Faith, your grand Mammy, and Nina, your great grand Mammy, was at one time everything I loved and all that I had. When the white man came, you know, those people who are the color of your little friend in there, Julia? Yeah, I know her name!" He broke into short laughter. "When they came and took my world, and all my people who I thought cared about me turned their backs on me, including your one-eyed grand mammy, I just had to take the pleasure of repaying them. I took from them the same things they took from me … everything! Now get outta my goddamn walls!"

He ended in a great baritone. Halting, he heard no response or movement. A crackling and breaking in the distance itched his hunger to kill. "What in the world?" Jamanny peeked into the entrance and flicked on his lighter, revealing the passageway. "Sneaky little rats! There's one thing I hate, ladies, and that's rats in my house!" He opened the entrance to his liking and squeezed inside, cracking the walls in some places.

Breaking through walls, fleeing through rooms of torture, Destiny ran off and hid inside the darkness. Faith and Julia split, hiding against a wall inside a large room. Staying low, they saw pools and splashes of blood everywhere, remembering the horror inflicted upon them.

"I don't hear him anymore. Where did he go?" Julia whispered, trying not to breathe so hard. As sweat poured from her drained body, she pressed her ear to the floor.

"I can't see anything." Faith's hand clasped against her spiky mouth. A small flicker of flame passed through the cracks in the wall behind them. The sound of Jamanny blowing it out sent Faith and Julia glancing into each other's wide, startled eyes.

Julia held up a finger between them, listening. Jamanny's fist burst through the eroding drywall and wood, connecting with the side of Julia's head.

Unable to hold up his gun, Jamanny came fully through the wall. Faith, in a windmill motion, thrashed him across the upper body with the chain. "Damn it, you bitch!"

An internal crunch and a bright flash of light pushed the old man back, leaving another front tooth missing. As he fired at Julia's dazed head, Faith knocked her to the floor, then by the ankles, dragged her by her feet into the next room.

Chasing them, Jamanny dodged a flying chair that broke to pieces inside the doorway. "Missed me!" A woman's taunting voice sent him blasting around the room. Seeing shadows, he chased them out into the main hall, firing two more as they disappeared around the corner into Junior's room. "I love cat and mouse! You can't run, and you certainly can't hide in my house forever!" He reloaded the gun and fired into the ceiling. "This is my house, and I make the rules! Come out and fight like your grand mammy! We could carve all your pretty little eyes right out of your faces—and make you just as beautiful as she was. I'll put them in a pretty pink jar; wouldn't you like that? It'll be fun!"

He moved like a secret agent toward the corner of the metal door that was normally shut, aiming his rifle in the clear. "Junior! Timmy?" He found it odd that Junior wasn't in his room. Noticing the door on the other side of the room slightly flapping, he followed the sound of running feet into the hallway. "Females." He fired at them over a familiar shape in the middle of the corridor. "I'm gonna send you heifers straight to heaven!" He saw them dashing out of a room, cutting the corner with Destiny, and shot into the dimness of uncertainty.

Penetrating the walls, part of Julia's arm was instantly exposed to the bone by the bullet. "Ah, he got me, girl!" She held her arm as Faith pulled her along. With no time to think, Faith kicked an opening through the nearest wall. "I can't believe we could have done this shit a long time ago!" Another blast from Jamanny's gun clipped the ends of Julia's hair.

"Where you off to now? Leaving so soon?" Jamanny approached another large hole in the wall. "You two are like regular groundhogs! Who's gonna pay for all this damage? I know, you—with your lives!" He filled the halls with flashes of light and the sound of thunder. Looking down, he felt one cartridge of ammunition left in his overall pocket. Patting seeping blood on his face, Jamanny scratched his nose and pointed the smoking barrel directly in front of him. "You don't want to be down here." A small arm bone snapped under his feet.

"This is for Big Momma!" Faith smacked his arm down with the rod, and Julia smashed a skull against his head. Feeling the tight straps of his trousers loosening, and the skin across his chest being severed by Julia's scythe, he hollered in pain. His ammo hit the floor.

More shots were fired, bringing Jamanny and Julia tussling over the rifle. Faith, in fear of their current position, stretched the chain with the other hand and leaped on his back. Choking him, Faith twisted the chain around his neck. He tossed and clawed for air. Using the rifle as a bat, Jamanny struck Julia in the midsection, launching her across the room. Flipping the gun in one hand, he fired over his shoulder, missing Faith again. Then, flipping her over his head, Jamanny pointed and pulled the trigger to the clicking sound of no bullets.

Faith and Julia broke through the nearest wall. "That's it, roaches— no more games. I'm coming to get ya!" He found the cartridge and loaded his last bullets into the chamber, locking the pin. "Round two." He limped desperately after the escapees. "It's too late for second chances now—and no time outs. I told you—you can't hide! I can smell your pussies a mile away! Mmm!"

Through the broken wood, he reentered the dark area, which was the center of the entire floor. Crunching bones of various species and people beneath his feet, Jamanny regained a proud strength, empowered by the remains of his enemies. On the far collapsing wall to the right, he spotted a new entrance that had been made by the trio. Walking to the hole gave another view to the hall and the room where Rashida was. He stooped and stepped through. Slowly coming to the door, whimpering, he stepped under the table next to Rashida's barely breathing body. He glanced at a pair of kneeling legs.

"Nina—or shall I say Destiny—poor baby. Daddy forgives you." Jamanny paused and slowly bent to get a better view of the scared child. Irritable and fed up, his red eyes saw her tiny body folded in a ball. "Aww, Mommy and her friend left you again? Tsk, tsk, tsk."

Holding out something in front of her, she flicked a blue flame from a small lighter. "You know, this is the occasion for a smoke. How's about I declare today your birthday?" Saluting her surrender, Jamanny reached for his cigar. Destiny revealed a can of aerosol spray that instantly became a flamethrower and launched a ball of fire into his face. Ducking backward, he headed for the door. Burning seared over his previous injuries, Jamanny and his fluttering heart met the blade of Julia's scythe as it cut three inches into his back.

"Fuck you!"

"Go to hell!" Faith jabbed the long twisting jagged rod through his eye, puncturing his brain.

Before he could scream or even react to the pain, he fell in the doorway in a slow, lengthy gurgle of blood, spit, and jumping nerves. Faith and Julia stood over his body like two battered Amazon warriors.

"Mommy." Destiny crawled from under the table and ran to her mother's side.

"It's over, baby; it's finally over." Faith unraveled the chain and dropped it on the floor.

"Let's get out of here." Julia stepped over Jamanny's body in the hall.

When Dozer saw his dead father, he grabbed her from the side and put a knife to her throat.

"Wait! Don't you do that. You're not like him. Don't you do that! Wait. Hold on! Just listen to me. Hear me out—and then make your choice!" Faith saw blood trickling from Julia's neck. "Now you wait a goddamn minute! This is your mother!" Faith pointed to Rashida. "Your father misled you; he lied to you! He made you do these things, but it doesn't have to be this way!"

"Dozer, listen! It's true; he was lying to us the whole time. This is my mother, and Rashida is yours! This whole thing is wrong, Dozer—and you know that!" Destiny moved in front of her mother.

"Listen to her, Dozer; this isn't right! You're not like him; it doesn't have to be this way. Look at what he made you do to them, to her, your own mother? Now she needs a doctor real bad. Dozer, change this … save her."

As Dozer lowered the knife, Faith sighed in relief, watching Pig and his two little brothers as they appeared behind him in the hall.

"I made it to the car—just like you told me. I found your phone and talked to that woman, Mary." Pig entered the room to see her mother. Passing Faith the phone, she stood between her and Destiny. "She told me to turn on something called a GPS."

As the children look at their deceased father, Rashida appeared to be dead. Approaching, in mixed emotions and confusion, Dozer keeled over her.

"Momma, I'm sorry, I'm sorry," Dozer said.

Pig and his two baby brothers gathered behind him, sprinkling tears down like a cool rain upon their mother's smiling face.

The End??

Song of the Hummingbird
THE OTHER ENDING

———— ✳ ————

Inside the clutter of the attic, two sheets of newspaper connecting Faith and Destiny to the murder of Jamondo blew out from the rectangular entrance. Having known where her father hid Faith's grandmother's shotgun, Tina lurched down the halls with a weapon in hand.

"Hi!" Holding her wrapped arm, Julia waved at the troubled, weeping teen. "Hey, what are ya doing with that? You don't need that! Faith?" After an explosion, a single shell dispersed pellets that traveled through the center of Julia's head, clearing her body from the doorway.

"Jay?" Faith yelled over the children's screams.

"Tina, what are you doing?" shouted Pig at the sight of her sister.

"Tina! No! This is your mom! Tina, she's here; what's wrong?" Destiny said as Faith used her own body as a shield.

"Put it down, Tina; put the gun down!" Dozer said as Tina allowed Lamond and Omack to run out.

"Please, it's over—no more killing! Let me be with my daughter; there's your mother!" Faith tried to talk sense into the girl. "Please, stop! Put that fuckin' gun down!"

"Shut up! Just close your mouths right now—all of you!" Tina hollered. "I know that's our fuckin' mother! She's a liar just like him!" The delirious teenager aimed at her deceased father and looked at Faith. "Bitch, you are right; it's over! It was over when you came here!"

"What's your goddamn problem?" Faith yelled.

Destiny said, "Tina, what's wrong?"

"What's the problem? What's wrong?" Tina became more agitated. "You don't get it, do you? You are the daughter of the murderer of my brother, that home-wrecker! You ain't no sister of mine. I ain't never liked you! Your mother, your own flesh and blood, fucked my man, had his baby, and killed him! I hate you! He was the father of my baby that Daddy killed! I loved him, you bitch! Fuck you and Daddy's house!"

"No, that's not true—that's not how it went!"

Multiple shots rang out. Two baby boys ran across the property, and the shadow of a young girl carrying a gun stepped out of the house. Running in the direction of the little boys, she stopped. A bright light and a loud bang filled and illuminated everything as her body folded and slumped to the earth.

At an oak tree by the roadside, two boys stood together, out of place. As the smallest one sat in the grass playing with pebbles, he glanced at Lamond—and then at a man walking toward them. The man was pushing a cart.

Dressed in tattered clothes, he used a stick as a cane. The hunchbacked man stopped and looked down at them. "Hey, I know you two! You're Jamanny's youngun's, aren't ya?" The two boys stared at him without saying a word. "I saw what happened at your house, a plum shame, a plum shame! Whewee! It's not too safe back there right now. Say, I have an idea. Wanna come with me? I could raise ya!" He smiled at the two boys. Standing up, they took hold of his cart and slowly walked away with him. "Say, I could tell you were Jamanny's boys. There's something about those weird cat eyes of yours. You look just like your brothers." The old man laughed, walking them down the dirt road.

Escorted by the homeless man, the boys in their overalls and T-shirts stopped by the grass. Lamond picked up a jagged piece of wood, pricking himself on its sharp edge. Sucking on his stinging finger, he turned to Omack. They looked back at the old black house in the distance. Full of hatred, suffering, and revenge, satisfied, slept the house upon its unstableness, burnt and bloodstained foundation. The tales of lost life and forgotten souls blow with the leaves across the night breeze. Against the celebrating swaying trees as if GOD lifted his hand from the darkness, screams of pain and uncensored cursing were replaced by peace and tranquility. Inside and beyond the yard, nature continued to slowly take back the land that man had abused and taken from it. Hungry and confused, with the pain in their hearts aching into memories that they carried on with them, boldly and bravely, two little boys went off into the uncertain future, like a humming bird carrying the tune of the last.

The End

Moral: Life doesn't always end in happy endings!